THE AMISH COWBOY'S REFUGE

AMISH COWBOYS OF MONTANA
BOOK VII

ADINA SENFT

Cover design by Carpe Librum Book Design. Images used under license. Song
92 from the *Ausbund* translated by Shelley Adina Senft Bates.

The Amish Cowboy's Refuge / Adina Senft—1st ed.

ISBN 978-1-950854-92-9 R022524

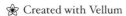 Created with Vellum

IN THIS SERIES

AMISH COWBOYS OF MONTANA

CAST OF CHARACTERS
THE AMISH COWBOY'S REFUGE

The Amish Cowboy's Refuge introduces a new branch of the Miller family, recently moved from their New Mexico ranch to Mountain Home, Montana. Rachel Miller is the widow of Marlon Miller, Reuben's brother. She is first cousin to the Zook brothers, Willard and Hezekiah (and yes, she too despairs of those two ever getting married).

The Millers at the Wild Rose Amish Inn

- Rachel Zook Miller
- Tobias Miller, widower, father of twins Gracie and Benny
- Gideon Miller
- Susanna Miller
- Seth Miller

The Millers on the Circle M Ranch

- Reuben and Naomi Glick Miller
- Daniel and Lovina Wengerd Lapp Miller, Joel
- Adam Miller and Kate Weaver (engaged)
- Zach Miller and Ruby Wengerd (engaged)
- Malena Miller and Alden Stolzfus (courting)
- Noah and Rebecca Miller King
- Joshua and Sara Fischer Miller, Nathan
- Deborah Miller (age 1)

THE AMISH COWBOY'S REFUGE

1

MOUNTAIN HOME, MONTANA

I will say of the Lord, He is my refuge and my fortress: my God; in him will I trust. —*Psalm 91:2*

Thursday, April 21

WITH THE SENSE of hope and optimism that comes with obedience to *Gott's wille*, Rachel Miller slid the sign into the wrought-iron holder that Alden Stolzfus had made in the new gate. "There."

WILD ROSE AMISH INN

"Looks a sight better than that faded shingle on a piece of baling wire," observed her cousin Willard Zook.

"You do *gut* work, Will." Rachel's gaze ran lovingly over the hand-carved and painted wild roses, pink with gold centers, like the ones that grew in the valley, and the fresh white lettering on moss green, to match the paint they'd use on the inn's doors and window frames once the weather warmed up.

Willard mumbled something about vanity and swelled heads, but she was having none of it.

"I'm only telling the truth. This sign welcomes people—it doesn't inform them they just got their last chance."

Which is what the name Tumbleweed's Refuge used to do, in her opinion. The place where tumbleweeds fetched up, because the wind couldn't leave them anywhere else. When she'd asked the library clerk to help her register the inn's new name with the county computer system, it had been a happy moment to have that old name erased and the name she'd given the place put in. It hadn't been such a happy thing to send the money for her innkeeper's license, mind you, but you had to take the good with the bad in this world, as *Gott* sent it.

"How about you give me a tour?" Willard said.

"Sure. We have about half an hour before the twins get home from school."

Willard groaned. "Better get a move on, then. How did a boy as solid as Tobias wind up with a pair of terrors like that?"

"They're not terrors," Rachel said indignantly as she led the way to the inn's front door. "They just need a mother. Susanna and I are doing what we can, but it's not the same."

"I told you what they did after church this past week, didn't I?"

"At least four times, Willard." It had only been a tiny round of goat cheese. They'd wanted to taste it—and had received their reward. The cheese needed to age, apparently, and the experience had been so awful that now the twins avoided the Zook dairy completely. So Will and Zeke had received their reward, too. "Are you coming?"

He'd got hung up outside. "You keeping this river rock base on the exterior walls?"

"I certainly am. It would cost a fortune to replace it. And

THE AMISH COWBOY'S REFUGE

it's solid." She ran a hand up the newly installed shake siding above the rock. "The county tells me the place was built at the turn of the century and I wanted it to look like it belongs. Only in better shape."

"It does that," he said, walking along the broad, welcoming covered porch as though he was inspecting Noah King's work.

She liked the Old West look of it, though now, thankfully, it was looking more west than old. "Come on in and see."

The sound of hammering and the men joshing back and forth came from upstairs. But down here, there was only her and her cousin. Once through the glassed-in mud room, the entry hall was open to the keeping room on the right and the guest dining room on the left. "We just got the floors laid. I think the hickory planks make it look warm and welcoming, don't you?"

"Smells like varnish."

Not for long. "This is where the guests will gather if they want to. I'll have comfortable sofas and a Thermos flask of coffee, and some baking set out across the way in the afternoons. Lots of books." She pointed. "We kept the river-rock fireplace, too. Daniel's built-in bookshelves look just right running along those two walls. And I even have a window seat." The bay window looked out on the parking lot, but the embrasure was nice and deep, with mullioned casements on either side. A person didn't look outside much when they were reading, anyway.

"You'll see the dining room leads straight back to the kitchen."

"I bet that was a mess." Willard ambled behind her, taking in every unputtied nail hole, she was sure.

"There were mice living in the stove. Noah gutted the whole thing and started over. We had to replace the wiring, of course, in case I ever sell it to an *Englisch* person, but the stove and refrigerator are propane." She didn't add that having brand-new appliances and a farm sink with a gooseneck faucet for the first time in her life was a secret thrill. Her sister-in-law Naomi understood, and they'd bounced and squealed like a couple of teenage girls when Noah had finished installing them.

"Back here are the family quarters," she went on. "Except for one bedroom there, right behind the keeping room, for a disabled or elderly guest. The rest of the guest rooms are all upstairs, but they're not finished yet. Reuben and Naomi encouraged us to stay at the Circle M as long as we needed, but I wanted the family quarters finished first, so we could get out of their hair."

"You call this finished?" Willard walked down the corridor, peering in at the empty rooms. Since she wouldn't be serving guests their supper, there a table and chairs in the family parlor for meals and prayer, and where the twins might do their homework and she could sew.

"These rooms have been plastered and painted," she retorted. "They have finished floors and windows. They haven't had the sawdust cleaned out yet, but they're done."

"When are you moving in?"

"This week, as it happens," she said. "Want to come and help?"

"Help what? You got furniture hidden somewhere?"

"As a matter of fact, we do. It's been in Reuben's barn since it arrived. I'll have to hire a truck to move it all over here."

Willard grunted. "That's what spring wagons are for. And hay wagons. Don't go wasting your money on *Englisch* vehicles, Rachel Miller."

Trying not to smile at his roundabout way of volunteering

his vehicles, she followed him up the stairs. "Like I said, not much to see up here."

"Hey!" came the mock-indignant chorus as her crew greeted Willard. They were sheathing the interior walls, and the windows were in, which meant they could start on the Sheetrock any day.

"Two of these rooms are bigger," Willard noted as they walked through.

"Folks will be paying for them to be bigger," she pointed out. "We knocked out the walls between some of the original ones to make a honeymoon suite here at the end, and a family suite back there, by the stairs."

He turned to look at her. "How big is this place?"

"What you see." She indicated the rough-cut rooms with both hands. "There are three guest rooms for couples along with the two big ones."

"You think hunters come in couples?"

She grinned at him. "They might. I've got beds on order. They're twin-sized that can be connected to make one king-size. I'm hoping for lots of hunters and fishermen, so I wanted to be able to sleep as many as I could."

He made a noise that might have been grudging agreement ... or dust in his throat.

At the end of the hall was a big window whose casements swung out. He gazed at the view of the field out back, a green belt full of pines and aspens, and then the roof of Yoder's Variety Store on the far side. "Where are you going to put your horses?"

"At the Circle M, for now."

"Reuben and I are organizing a barn raising on the first of June," Noah called from one of the rooms. "You might spread the word, Willard."

"We figure we might get some attention for the inn that way," Rachel went on. "Maybe the *Englisch* haven't seen a barn raising here. This isn't a ranch, but Noah is still going to build a bunkhouse over it, in case we get working cowboys who need a place to stay for a season. I'd charge them monthly room and board."

Willard eyed her. "Got this all figured out, haven't you?"

She made a short, disbelieving sound. "Me—and Reuben and Noah and Simeon and Tobias and my *Kinner*. Mostly all I do is say *ja* or *neh* to whatever they propose."

"I'm thinking you're pretty glad that Noah King decided to marry your niece."

Noah leaned out of the room he was working on. "Noah King is pretty glad about that, too."

She led Willard back down the stairs and lowered her voice. "You might think Simeon King is the brains of the outfit, but Noah really runs the outfit. He's going to start on his own house once we move in here. Which reminds me, Willard. You know our northeast field backs on to your southwest property line."

"Does it?" he said in the tone that told her he knew perfectly well, and could probably tell her the number of fence posts he had to maintain between them, too.

"Aendi Annie King's place is a good size, but not for building houses and growing hay for young folk getting married and settling down. I was thinking of deeding Noah and Rebecca that lot in lieu of what I owe him for his work here. It's an odd shape, but there's enough room for a house and a shop, and it's got county road frontage on one side."

Cousin Willard gazed at her. Silently. She couldn't read his expression.

"Just think it over," she said. "I've said nothing to anyone yet, not even Noah. Or Tobias. But I would like your advice on it, and Hezekiah's too."

"Seems like you'd want to deed it to one of your own boys," he finally said. Clearly this had been behind the silence all along.

"My sons are cowboys, not carpenters," she pointed out. "And we've only been here since February. Who knows if they'll find work in the valley, or have to move on to eastern Montana or Colorado or even Alberta?"

"Still."

"If they're going to settle on a ranch in the Siksika, it would have to be one already operating here. You know that. They'd need to go in on it as partners, like Reuben's *Kinner* are with him. That little piece of land between us isn't going to benefit my sons unless they decide to take up machinery conversions or something. And I haven't seen any tendencies in that direction."

Willard merely nodded. "We'll talk it over, Zeke and me. I'll let you know what he thinks in a few days." He thought for a moment. "Not after church. No business on the Lord's day. But maybe you all might come for supper some night. If all four of your *Kinner* spend the evening chasing those baby coyotes disguised as children, the three of us might get a chance to have a word together."

He ambled toward the door. She did her best to forgive the insult to her good-hearted, curious grandchildren as she glanced out the window. She was rewarded with the welcome sight of Gracie and Benny clambering down from the Keim buggy across the highway at the new feed store. At seven, they were old enough to walk the mile to the Circle M from school. But sometimes, when they wanted to see their father and help a little before they all went back to the ranch together, someone would give them a ride over, as Sylvia Keim had done.

"Speaking of, here they are," she said brightly.

Willard picked up his pace, and by the time she made it downstairs, all she saw of him was a hand waving out the window of the buggy. He flapped the reins over his horse's back and made the wide turn out of the parking lot and over the bridge onto Creekside Lane with indecent haste.

When the children ran across the bridge to meet her at the gate, she was still laughing.

"Mammi, what's so funny?" Gracie demanded, flinging her arms around her in a hug as tight as if they hadn't seen each other in months.

"I'm just happy." She indicated the new sign. "Look what Cousin Willard made for us. Isn't it pretty?"

"*Ja!*" And they were off again, the apples of her eyes. Then Benny skidded to a stop and pulled something out of the deep pockets of his black wool coat. "I forgot. Sylvia stopped at the post office and there was a bunch of mail."

She barely had time to get her hands around it before he took off to see what the carpenters had got done today, his book satchel bouncing on his back.

She walked slowly into the inn, sorting through what had been forwarded from the Ventana Valley post office in New Mexico, and what had come to the Inn's box here, both for her and for the previous owner. Junk, junk, circular, *The Budget*, oh good—a big fat envelope that no doubt held the circle letter from her buddy bunch. She was the last one in the circle now, the farthest west, which meant she got everybody's news before she started a fresh one with all the news of her own. Here was a letter from their former bishop in New Mexico, no doubt giving his forwarding address and letting her know they were packed up and on their way back to Shipshe.

As she went to toss the junk mail in the big metal garbage skip the carpenters had put outside, a postcard fell out of the circular.

Santa Fe, New Mexico Welcomes You. A collage of chile ristras and the Plaza. She turned it over and saw the handwriting that she always recognized no matter how many years passed betweentimes.

Was sorry to miss you all. Nice place you had here. Bishop says you sold up and moved back to the Siksika. My family's all gone from there now, but I wonder if anyone could use a wrangler, what with shots and branding coming up. Maybe I could stop in and see. Hope that's all right.

Luke Hertzler

Friday, April 22

"WELL, OF ALL THINGS." Naomi had taken Rachel upstairs to show her the quilt that Malena was laying out, and Rachel had seized the opportunity to show her sister-in-law the postcard in her apron pocket. From below they could hear the chatter of voices as Malena and Rebecca and Kate Weaver did the dishes, while Susanna fed her one-year-old cousin Deborah. A yell came from the basement, right up through the heat vent. Poor Zach was putting wood in the woodstove, and clearly Benny objected to his methods.

"That's two postcards within a couple of months, after ten or fifteen years of silence," Rachel said unnecessarily, as Naomi turned it over to look at the pictures. She'd written to tell Naomi about the first one after Christmas.

"The man's probably lonely."

Together, they stood to admire the blocks of the quilt top, which would be a cluster of lupines on a pieced background that suggested a meadow and clouds.

Naomi glanced at her. "I suppose you've heard the talk."

A pleat formed between Rachel's brows, which she made a conscious effort to smooth away. "Not a lot of talk going around in the Ventana Valley anymore. The bishop has all he can do to open his mouth to preach. He's so shy that gossip is beyond him."

"Not lately," Naomi said. "I mean, from years back. About Luke's family."

Rachel nodded slowly. "Just a hint. A whisper or two. Something about his wife and *Kinner*, and whatever happened to them being his fault. Honestly, Naomi, in those years when the *Kinner* were growing up, and later, when I was learning to manage the ranch alone, if someone didn't write about it in a circle letter, then I didn't hear it. And in a letter, you know, you're a little more circumspect than you would be just talking about something over the garden fence. Especially in a circle like ours, with a dozen people in it."

"It's not the same as a quilting frolic," Naomi said by way of agreement. "He's welcome to stay here, of course."

"That's kind of you. But we're moving into the Inn in a few days. He can stay with us. When he turns up. If he does."

"Do you think that's wise?" Naomi's voice was gentle, but she was reining in all she really wanted to say. Rachel could tell.

"If I want to get the Inn finished by the time the rivers open, it is." Rachel felt rather than saw Naomi's start of surprise. "Luke used to swing a hammer some. I expect he hasn't lost the knack. And if the weather starts warming up, Noah's going to get busy, and less likely to want to push out a big job offer just to do all our finish work."

"That wouldn't be like Noah," Naomi protested.

"You know how fiddly and time-consuming it is. Both of us have helped to build houses and puttied our share of nail holes.

I can pay Noah to install wainscoting and crown molding and varnish banisters, or he can move on and Luke and my sons can do it."

"For room and board?"

"*Ja*, and maybe more, if his work is good. The laborer is worthy of his hire. And as you read, he's looking for work."

"I wonder," Naomi said under her breath.

Rachel gave her the look that her children understood to mean, *Out with it.*

"About why he's really coming. Why he's following you around the West all of a sudden, after what amounts to a lifetime."

Rachel wondered that herself. "You said it—maybe he's lonely. He used to live here, too, remember? He had friends."

"Wasn't that how Marlon knew him? He was palling around with Willard and Hezekiah and some of the other young men."

Rachel nodded. "They were inseparable growing up—whenever you saw the one, you saw the other."

"Except on dates with Marlon, presumably," Naomi said with a smile. "A few years later."

Rachel turned a little to admire the quilt from a different angle, so her sister-in-law couldn't see her face. "*Ja*. Marlon didn't like to double date."

And except when Rachel snuck off to see Luke. Which no one knew about. Not then, and not now.

Tobias and his two brothers took the twins down to Daniel and Lovina's, where they were bunking during the renovations. The twins walked to school with Joel, who might be only two years older, but to whom they looked up with awe. She gathered it was something to do with being able to rope a calf, which they weren't allowed to try yet. Now, the big house settled into quiet as everyone went to bed. The wind was blowing in from the northeast, as cold as if it were January. But inside, the house was cozy and the window quilts thick, muffling the wind's attempts to get in.

Rachel brushed her teeth and took down her hair, still thick and nut-brown even if it had gone gray in a ribbon on either side of her face. She slipped on her nightgown and sat on the guest bed, turning the postcard over to read it again by the warm glow of the kerosene lamp.

Luke Hertzler.

She wished she could remember what had happened to him. Or rather, his wife and their two children. But life had been hard after Marlon's death, and anything that wasn't related to her own children's or the cows' survival took a backseat and eventually fell away. Her memories of their shared past were clearer. Much clearer, in the way guilty secrets tended to be. He'd been fun to be with—good-looking, too, with a pair of eyes that could make a girl wish she hadn't been quite so well brought up.

Rachel shook her head at that girl she'd been. Seeing two boys at the same time, even though they were best friends. How had she managed it? To this day, all she could remember were endless arrangements designed to keep them apart, and a sense of thankfulness that of all things, those two boys didn't talk about who they were dating. Granted, not many of the Amish did. The teasing could be awful, which was why sometimes even parents didn't know who their sons or daughters were seeing until they announced their engagement.

Like Tobias. Rachel had been completely in the dark until he and Lily Anne had walked out to the garden, where she'd been watering the chile plants, and she'd seen they were holding hands.

It hadn't come to that with Luke, because late in that crazy summer, the scales had tilted in Marlon's favor—Marlon, with his years of experience in ranching with his father, and some cousins in the Rio Ventana country who had let him know some good ranch land was coming available. He'd asked her to marry him on her birthday in September. Their wedding had been an emotional ride on a bucking bronc—sitting with her *Neuwesitzern* across from Marlon, Reuben, and Luke and feeling the gaze of the latter upon her the length of the entire ceremony. As though he thought she might still change her mind, right up there in front of God and the bishop and everyone.

She hadn't, and she'd never regretted it. Those thoughts during those early years couldn't really be called regret. She took her vows seriously, so she'd bundled up the man and the thoughts both, and locked them in a room in her heart.

But sometimes, when she and Marlon had had a disagreement, or she'd had some disappointment, she might tiptoe into that secret room and pull out a memory. Become a girl again, looking into those eyes and feeling a temptation she could never give in to. Hear the sound of the river in their secret place in the woods, listening to the music in his voice as they talked long into the night, cuddled up against him. But then she'd put those memories away, turn the key in her mind, and go back out into her life to deal with what *der Herr* had put before her.

In the end, memories couldn't sustain a person. They were like a diet of cake, and you didn't turn down good beef and healthy vegetables to live on cake, did you? Real life sustained a woman—her children, her home, and her healthy love for her *Mann*. Rachel had learned that lesson, and to the best of her knowledge, to the day he died Marlon had never known about her and Luke, or about the secret room in her heart that she'd allowed to grow increasingly dusty and neglected as the years passed.

She didn't deserve *Gott*'s mercy in keeping it from the man she had loved and married. But even now, she was grateful for it.

Tuesday, April 26

"Mammi! It's moving day!" Gracie ran into the Circle M kitchen full tilt, shedding her black wool coat, her mittens, and her black away bonnet on the way. Rachel turned from the stove just in time to catch her in a hug while Naomi rescued the pan of sizzling eggs.

"*Ja*, it is, *Liewi*. Better pick up your things or Onkel Reuben and Zach and Adam will tread on them when they come in for breakfast."

The twins might move at top speed, but their obedience came just as quickly. Most of the time. Gracie scooped up her coat and other belongings and hung them in the mud room as her brother and father came in with Seth and Gideon. Daniel, Lovina, and Joel followed, for this was their last family breakfast together. And true to form, the kitchen filled with chatter and laughter as everyone found a chair around the tables that had been pushed together and covered with checked oilcloth.

Rachel was used to cooking for her own family and the ranch hands, but she didn't think she'd ever get tired of a Circle M spread. She and Naomi had begun last night, compiling the sweet potato casseroles and preparing the sausage for the gravy. Now everyone had biscuits and gravy, hot coffee, scrambled cheesy eggs, and a celebratory jar of red chile salsa from Rachel's last batch made on the Four Winds Ranch.

After cleanup and dishes, the twins left for school with

Joel, just in time to meet Willard and Hezekiah in the lane at the reins of a spring wagon and a hay wagon, respectively. She shared a grin with Naomi. The Amish were economical—some might even say frugal—with their money, but her cousins were just plain cheap.

Not that she was complaining. She hadn't really wanted to rent a moving van, even a small one. So every wagon and every pair of hands was welcome this morning. Especially those of the twins, who had been given the day off school for the occasion.

One after the other, the family's wagons and buggies filled with the furniture, boxes, and possessions from New Mexico. Zach and Adam even hitched Hester to Rachel's buggy, and Rachel's and Susanna's suitcases and bags from the house went into it. While they made quite the parade down the county highway, with all the help they could do it in a single trip. Anything left behind could be collected during visits after church, or dropped by on a trip to town for groceries.

Her job was to holler instructions and direct where things were to go after everything was unloaded in the parking lot at the inn. "Watch out for the mud!" Susanna cried. "Zach, don't drop my dresser!"

Zach and Adam didn't have the breath to reply as they carried in the antique dresser that had once belonged to Rachel's grandmother. It was hand carved and pretty, and held nearly every stitch of clothing Susanna owned, but it was also heavy, even with the drawers taken out.

In came the kitchen table and chairs, and boxes filled with dry goods, silverware, all the linens, and goodness knew what else. Their beds went down the short corridor in pieces, the mattresses and box springs after them. Somewhere there was a box full of sheets and pillowcases, but she hadn't seen it yet. Here was the sofa and the two armchairs. "In the keeping room, please—oh! Wait! That big Navajo rug has to go down first. It's rolled up in Willard's wagon with its underlay."

Willard found the rug, and it took both brothers to carry it in. But as many miles as it had traveled, it suited the room perfectly, and the sofa and chairs, too. "It looks great, Mamm," Seth said quietly, breathing hard after wrestling mattresses into submission. "I'll be glad to see our books and pictures again."

She spotted Zach coming out of the guests' dining room after depositing a pair of chairs, and raised her voice a little as she spoke to Seth. "I'm hoping that one of your cousins will draw something to hang in the dining room."

Zach smiled his quiet smile, and Ruby Wengerd, who had driven the bishop's spring wagon, came up behind him and leaned on his shoulder. In the folds of her dress, their fingers twined together. "I'm hoping that, too," she said to him. "A view of the valley, maybe?"

"Maybe," he said easily, then glanced at Rachel. "Or I could draw the Four Winds ranch house from memory. As a keepsake."

Part of her wanted him to, in memory of the happy life she and Marlon had built there. But part of her wanted to look to the future, not the past.

"You know what I'd really like?" she mused aloud. "A picture of the wild roses growing along the fence. You could do them in colors, like the one you did of the sandhill cranes that one Christmas."

"You don't think that's overdoing it, Mamm?" Seth asked skeptically. "Live ones outside and sketched ones inside?"

"If you were a hunter's wife, curled up by the fire in October waiting for your man to come back with his elk, you might not think so. You might appreciate the reminder that summer will come again, no matter how cold it gets."

Seth laughed. "I guess that settles it. Get out your pink pastels, Zach."

But her nephew met her eyes with pleasure at the prospect. "Happy to. I'm pretty fond of summer myself—and everyone is glad to see the wild roses. But now I have to go. I'm on call today, so I'd best get back home."

Both Zach and Adam were volunteer firemen—Adam had gone a step further and received his EMT license thanks to long hours of studying and his sister-in-law Sara's coaching.

When the wagons were empty and the furniture placed mostly where she wanted it, Rachel unpacked the hamper of rolls, banana cake with cream cheese frosting, and the little savory tarts that she'd prepared for a midmorning snack. Zach and Ruby carried theirs with them as they tied Hester behind the bishop's wagon and headed the five miles back to the Circle M. Gideon located the rest of the chairs on the porch— not in the mud, thank goodness—and her family and her Zook cousins settled around the dining room table with a sense of relief.

"I can hardly believe it," Susanna said, looking around her at the clean bare walls and the big braided rug from the bunkhouse they'd laid under the table. "We're home."

"We are," Rachel agreed, "and soon our guests will be, too. I need to find the calendar so I can cross off the days until May twentieth."

"What's May twentieth?" Zeke wanted to know. "Besides the day before the rivers open."

"Think about it, *Bruder*," Willard said patiently. "Where are the fishermen going to lay their heads before they start keeping Amish hours on the river?"

Realization broke over Hezekiah's face. "Ah. Opening day of the inn."

Rachel smiled at him. "By my reckoning, we have twenty-four days to get this place finished and ready for guests."

Gideon groaned and buried his nose in his coffee mug. At least those had been easy to find. She still didn't know where the cutlery had gone.

"We'll do it, Mamm," Susanna said. "Noah said he can give us another two weeks, but we might lose Simeon if that property he's been looking at comes on the market. He says they're almost ready to sell. This past winter apparently was the last one the man's wife was willing to spend in Montana."

Willard snorted. "They spent five years saying they were fixing it up and not doing a thing. No wonder the wind was blowing in sideways. I hope Simeon King drives a hard bargain. He'll have it renovated in no time."

"He will with that Bontrager girl at the reins," mumbled Hezekiah.

"Nothing wrong with a good manager," Rachel informed the two confirmed bachelors over a pair of imaginary glasses. "Seems to me those two suit one another, and if *Gott* has brought them to each other, that's all that matters."

She would have said more, but a knock came at the door.

"I'll get it." Seth pushed back his chair. "Someone must have forgotten something."

"Or brought something we forgot," Susanna said.

"If it's a customer, tell them we'll be open on the twentieth," Rachel said, and reached for another piece of cake.

She heard the door open. Heard Seth greet the visitor in *Deitsch*, not *Englisch*.

And then she heard a voice she hadn't heard in a lifetime, and her piece of cake fell with a plop right into her coffee.

WILD ROSE AMISH INN

LUKE HERTZLER WAS PRETTY SURE the sign on the highway had said, MOUNTAIN HOME, MONTANA, POP. 2307. But as he'd climbed stiffly off the bus and collected his saddle and duffel bag from underneath, he would never have recognized the place.

When he'd left a lifetime ago, heartsore and disappointed, there had been nothing but a gas station, a bar, and a couple of stores, stranded in the middle of ranch country. The town was only there because it was on the old cattle-drive route from the previous century, and they'd watered at the confluence of the creek and the Siksika River. Cattle were still ambling into the bar's parking lot, because back then, there had been nothing to stop them. But something must have happened, because here was a main street straight out of a picture post-card, with swinging signs and names like Yoder's Variety Store and the Rose Garden Quilt Shop and the Bitterroot Dutch Café that told him the Amish folk had made the town their own. And in doing so, they'd clearly brought in the tourists, waving their money and happy to part with it.

He hoped the ranch owners were doing as well, and would feel inclined to hire a hand with a few miles on him, but lots of experience. Heaven knew he didn't have much else to his name. The man who had rented a fairly prosperous farm in Wisconsin, the man who had been a husband and father, who had welcomed the *Gmay* to his home of a Sunday, was no more. Vanished as completely as if he'd died. He'd asked *der Herr* a time or two if He'd grant that mercy, but He'd seen fit to turn a deaf ear and keep him around. Pared down to his bare essence. Owning nothing but what he could carry. A man who now considered himself prosperous if an employer paid on time and in cash.

Luke Hertzler hadn't had a home or a bank account in a decade at least. No point, when there was nothing to put in either one. Grief and guilt weren't exactly what you'd stuff into a safe deposit box, but they were the only things he was rich in.

He'd walked over to where the old stagecoach inn used to be, his boot heels clunking on the wooden bridge over the creek, and from the middle of the short span, got a look at what was there now. He pulled a piece of paper from his pocket and checked the address written in the bishop's careful hand.

This was the place. It still looked vaguely like Tumbleweed's Refuge, but in nearly all other ways was completely different. The difference between something deserted and dead, and something vitally alive. A split rail fence that needed half its rails replaced ran around what would be a broad lawn in the summer. The river rock base of the building was intact, but scrubbed to within an inch of its life. Where peeling planks had been, sporting the remains of oxblood paint, there was now fresh shingle siding—a new wraparound porch—new windows with the frames painted the shade of green approved by the *Ordnung*. The bishop had told him the truth—Rachel Miller had bought an inn and was in the midst of the grandmother of all renovations.

Luke had got his feet moving, down Creekside Lane and across the second bridge into the parking lot. The sign was brand new: WILD ROSE AMISH INN. A nice bit of work. Will Zook used to carve some back when they were kids, but he was probably long gone—dead or moved away.

It had taken everything in him to raise his hand and knock on a door so new its green paint gleamed. A young man answered it and he got his first look at Rachel's eyes in a stranger's face. The feeling of unreality he'd had all morning, coming back here—like a ghost walking through a place it was tied to, not touching anything, not being touched—cleared away in an instant when he saw those gentian-blue eyes.

The young man spoke; it took him some seconds to answer. The last time he'd spoken was in the Ventana Valley, thanking the bishop for the few dollars he'd earned helping him pack up. Just enough for bus fare here.

"Is this the Miller place?" he asked, to make sure. "I'm looking for Rachel Miller."

"That's my mother," the young man said, shaking his hand and pulling him inside at the same time. "I'm Seth Miller. Come on in."

She stepped out of a room on the left looking as though she'd seen the ghost he'd turned into. "Luke."

Her voice was the same as he remembered. Maybe a little huskier. The voice he'd heard music in, especially when she laughed. She'd changed—no longer the gangly girl, she was a tall, neat woman who held herself with authority. Beneath the starched white *Kapp*, he glimpsed hair that carried two matching streaks of gray.

Those eyes hadn't changed one bit, though, other than to gather a laugh line or two. He was glad about that.

She was waiting for him to say something. "*Guder mariye*, Rachel." Belatedly, he pulled off his battered brown Stetson. "I wrote."

"I got it. Come have some *Kaffee*. We just moved in this morning."

Surprise prickled through him. Where had they been in the months since they'd left the Ventana country if they just moved in?

The dining room held no furniture but the table and chairs, and all but one seat was full. Seth pressed him into it and told him he had work to do and not to worry. Magically, a hot cup of black coffee appeared in front of him, as well as a clean piece of paper towel and a piece of cake that tasted like ambrosia on his tongue.

"Well, as I live and breathe," said the old-timer across the table. "Luke Hertzler."

It took a good ten seconds before Luke could place that voice, and he sat back in astonishment. "Will? Willard Zook?" His gaze moved to the right. "And Hezekiah? I thought you'd be long gone. Or dead."

"Same." Hezekiah hadn't changed in that respect, at least. Said as little as possible until he made up his mind about something. Then he always had an opinion.

"Luke, this is my family," Rachel said. "My oldest son Tobias is twenty-eight, and these are his twins, Grace and Benjamin. Next to them is my *Dochsder* Susanna, and my middle boy, Gideon. You met Seth, the youngest boy."

Gideon had Marlon's eyebrows and determined chin.

Susanna might resemble Rachel's mother just a bit, but he wouldn't know for sure until she smiled. Which she didn't seem inclined to do. She merely nodded, watching him as if she'd never seen a cowboy before.

The mother of the twins didn't seem to be in the room. Maybe she was about somewhere, at work, like Seth.

"I—I was sorry to hear about Marlon, Rachel. I got wind of it some years back and meant to write, but..."

She seated herself at the right hand of the head of the table, though there was no chair there, no plate. But he could see Marlon's sturdy form there as clear as could be, and her in the wife's place as though she still held him to be head of the family.

"It's all right," she said. "It was hard losing him. Hard living without him. But *Gott* saw us through."

"And now you've come back."

"So have you." Her lashes flicked up, then fell again. "You were in the Ventana—you saw. The Amish families left one by one. When the preacher and the deacon did, too, we knew it was only a matter of time until we'd have to go."

"I gave the bishop a hand packing up. They got the train back to Shipshewana, and I got the train to Libby. I wouldn't have recognized Mountain Home if I hadn't seen the sign on the highway from the bus."

"You used to live here?" Tobias asked, removing what was clearly a second or third piece of cake from his son's sticky fingers.

"I did. I was one of your father's *Neuwesitzern*. Me and Reuben Miller."

Three pairs of eyes widened. "How come we've never heard of you?" Susanna blurted, then blushed scarlet. "Sorry, that didn't come out right."

"I'm sure you must have," Rachel said easily. "We used to tell our wedding story a lot when you were small."

"Wedding stories aren't so easy once you've had a loss," Willard pointed out. "So I'd imagine, anyway."

When Luke gazed at him, puzzled, Will went on, "Me and Zeke here, we've never married."

Now it was Luke's turn to be astonished. But it wasn't his place to ask questions. These men might have been his friends thirty years ago, but there had been a lot of water under the bridge since then. "What do you do for work?" When in doubt, ask a man his trade.

The Zook brothers looked at one another, then at him. "We keep a few goats and sheep. Make a lot of cheese," Willard said. "Help out where we're needed. We get by."

"You made that sign out front," he said, his hunch confirmed.

Willard looked pleased. "A housewarming gift for my cousin here."

"What do you do?" Hezekiah wanted to know. "Where's your home? Your family?"

Rachel's hands moved slightly, as though she wanted to shush him, before she stilled them.

"My saddle and gear are out on the porch," Luke replied. "I spent some years in Wisconsin. My folks passed away there, and my brothers and sister moved to various communities in Ohio and Indiana. Haven't heard from them in a long time. It's hard when I'm always on the move."

"Huh." Hezekiah eyed him.

Don't say it. Don't ask about my own family. They'd probably heard what happened years ago, but that didn't mean he was prepared to talk about it. To stave it off, he said, "I was hoping that with spring turnout, I'd be able to hire on somewhere."

"We were hoping to hire on at the Circle M," Gideon said. "With Joshua married and living on Sara's place, Reuben is down a hand. With us, he wouldn't need to hire any *Englisch*."

So Rachel had brought up a family of cowboys, just as her bishop had said. She'd done well for herself on the Four Winds Ranch, and sold it at a profit. Well, there had never been any moss on Rachel.

"Reuben's running the home place now," she said, in case he hadn't figured out the connection. "There are plenty of outfits looking for hands. The Rocking Diamond. The Keims are branding and tagging now, Reuben and the Bontragers plan to start Thursday. But—"

Seth wandered back in, a hammer in his hand. "But instead of helping out, we have to stay here and finish this place."

"Opening day is the twentieth," Susanna put in, but whether it was a reminder for her brother or information for him, Luke couldn't tell.

"You're going to make these boys bang nails instead of helping with branding?" Willard said to his cousin in surprise. "I wouldn't have thought that of you, Rachel, when every hand is needed."

"I'm not making anybody do anything," she retorted. "I know what the ranch outfits need. I also know what the Inn needs, if anybody hopes to have food in their bellies a month from now." She stood and began to collect the paper towels that had made do as plates. "Do you still swing a hammer, Luke?"

This was a morning for surprises. Why would she ask him that? "Not in a while," he said cautiously. "But I don't suppose I've lost the knack."

"How do you feel about giving us a hand here, then? If Tobias, Gideon, and Seth are set on branding, that leaves

Susanna and me on our own. And I'm probably as good at installing crown molding as you are at baking a cake." To punctuate this truth, she offered him the last of the savory tarts in the plastic container.

He took it before Benny got any ideas.

"I'll stay, Mamm," Tobias said.

"Not unless you pick up a hammer, too," she retorted. "If you're going to support your *Kinner*, you need a job with proper pay. You're not an innkeeper, Tobias. I made this choice to make a home for you and Benny and Gracie, and your brothers and sister, like the Four Winds was."

"You mean we're really not going home?" Little Benny looked as though this was the first time the notion had dawned on him.

"I know it felt like a visit, having Christmas at the Circle M, and starting school from there, but this is home now," his father told him. "It'll look more like it when we have a barn, and our horses come over from the ranch to be with us, too."

The boy looked around at the bare room, the boxes piled up across the hall, the lack of plates. "It doesn't look very much like home."

"It will, *Liewi*," Rachel assured him. Then she turned her attention back to Luke. "Do you need some time to think about it?"

If he could have smiled, he would have. But it was all he could do not to break down at her unexpected kindness. "*Neh*. I'd be happy to give you a hand, if you could recommend someplace I could stay."

One fine eyebrow rose. "You'd stay here. Where else?"

Susanna made a noise, and even Tobias looked surprised. "Here, Mamm?"

Willard got to his feet. "A room for the hired hand is a

room less for paying guests. Luke can stay with us and walk over every day. It's only a mile or so along the creek. Not too bad—unless we get a late snow."

Rachel jammed her hands on her hips. "You're my cousin, Willard Zook, not my husband."

Hezekiah rose, too. "It ain't fitting, Rachel. A lone wrangler staying in the house here with you?"

"And my four children and two grandchildren," she snapped.

Oh, Rachel was a sight when she was riled! At the same time, there was no way on earth that Luke would allow his presence to make her life awkward. Or for her to become the subject of talk. He knew better than anyone in this room how harmful that could be.

"Zeke's right, Rachel," he said. "I'd be grateful for the work if it will help you open on time and free up your sons for cowboyin'. If it's all right with you, I'll breakfast with your cousins and eat with you all here. I can keep working into the evening, too, if it won't disturb you."

"It won't disturb me a bit. We've had a few long days around here already, and only twenty-four left to go. But—"

"That's settled, then," Willard said, screwing down his black felt Siksika style hat on his head. "I can't promise the food will be as good at our place as you'll get here, Luke, but you won't starve."

Luke felt it best not to mention the number of times he'd done just that—or close enough. "When do you want me to start, Rachel?"

"Now," she said simply. "Maybe you can help us get unpacked and organized. I need to find my plates. Otherwise, you'll be getting your beef stew on a paper towel, too."

＊ + ＊

As she unpacked box after box in the kitchen, Rachel had to shake her head at herself. Memory was a treacherous thing. And when real life walked in—well, how silly could a woman be, half expecting the same good-looking flirt from thirty years ago? Luke Hertzler looked exactly like an abandoned creature that might have crept out of the sagebrush ... or out of the dusty, deserted room in her heart.

Older. Used up. Hanging onto life and hope by his fingernails.

The years had been hard on him, for sure and certain. She'd take pleasure in feeding him up a bit, if only she could find her plates.

"Here they are, Mamm," Susanna called from the keeping room. A moment later, she lugged in the heavy box with FIESTA clearly marked on the side in felt pen.

"Ach, denki," Rachel said on a breath of relief. For one horrible minute there, she thought she might have left them in New Mexico. "I've got all the shelves lined, so let's fill them. What are the men doing?"

"Building beds."

Of course they were, from the racket down the hall. "We'd better get our sheets matched up, or we'll be sleeping on bare mattresses."

Before they left, they'd washed all the dishes and packed them in clean pillowcases and bed sheets. Now it became almost a game, filling the glass-fronted cream cupboards with her Fiesta ware plates and bowls the colors of New Mexico—red, yellow, sky blue, and turquoise—and then matching up sets of bedding.

As she and her daughter folded sheets lengthwise and walked them together, Susanna said, "Where were you going to put Luke if he'd stayed, Mamm?"

"In the downstairs guest room for now." She gave the folded sheet a pat and stacked it with its fitted sheet. The pillowcases had to be here somewhere. "There isn't anyplace else. Why?"

"I just wondered. Zeke and Willard had a *gut* solution. He'll be more comfortable over there with old friends instead of in our mess."

"He's a wrangler," Rachel pointed out. "You know how they are—they come in the spring and leave in the fall, sleeping in an RV or a bunkhouse if they're lucky, in a tent if they're not. Not too many men in that line of work can afford to be fussy."

"I know, but ... he was Dat's *Neuwesitzer*. His best friend, *nix?*"

"*Ja*, he was. Willard and Hezekiah were a couple of years older, but they were his friends, too. You're right. It's *gut* for him to be with them again." She kept her voice measured, not loud, since the subject of their conversation was just down the corridor.

"Like you."

Rachel met Susanna's gaze, puzzled. What was she getting at?

And then Benny poked his head into the kitchen. "Beds are ready, Mammi. I put my own together. Dat only helped with the mattress. Why are mattresses so heavy?"

"Because they have springs and things inside to hold you up." Rachel ruffled his hair and picked up the stack of sheets. "Let's get your bed made. Do you know where your blanket and quilt are?"

He looked alarmed, his dark blue eyes fringed with sooty lashes the image of his father's. And hers, she supposed. *"Neh."*

"I'll find them," Susanna said. "I found the plates, so I think I can find your blankets, too."

Benny could make his own bed, but it was more fun doing it together. Gracie's was next, and then after the pillowcases turned up, they made their father's next door. Seth and Gideon shared a room, Susanna had her own small one, and Rachel's was next to the sewing room, which backed on to their little family parlor.

At length Luke appeared in the doorway with a stack of blankets and quilts so tall he was holding them in place with his chin. "Is this what you're looking for?"

"Ja!" Benny exclaimed. "That gray blanket goes on my bed, and the black quilt with the big purple diamond in the middle. Mammi made it for me out of shirts and stuff."

"Goodness, put them down before you drop them," Rachel told Luke. "The beds look *gut. Denki* for helping assemble them."

"Seth seemed to know where they went," Luke said mildly. "Did you make all these quilts?"

"Me and Susanna. *Gut* winter projects." Rachel handed Gracie her wool blanket and the matching black quilt with a diamond set on point in all the shades of green that their old shirts and dresses could yield. The little girl raced off to spread them on her bed.

"Now it's starting to look like home," came from their room. "Where's our rug?"

"Out here," their father called from the keeping room. "Mamm, isn't this sideboard supposed to be in the dining room?"

"What move ever goes smoothly?" she asked Luke whimsically. "At least everything arrived ... eventually."

"You've been at the Circle M since you got here?" Luke asked as he came out to give Tobias a hand with the sideboard. "How is Reuben? He married Naomi Glick, didn't he?"

"*Ja*, and they have six *Kinner*. The oldest, middle, and youngest are married. We had a *wunderbaar* Christmas wedding for Rebecca, the elder of the twins in the middle."

"More twins?"

"They run in the Millers. Marlon's mother was a twin."

"I'd forgotten." He grunted as he picked up one end of the sideboard and they manhandled it into the dining room.

"Under the window, *denki*," she called. "Susanna, bring that roll of shelf liner. We'll put both sets of china in it, for the guests, and then maybe we'll find my bedding, too."

The rest of the morning and the entire afternoon was a busy hum of work broken only by sandwiches for lunch. For a man who seemed so alone, Luke worked well with her brood. Not surprising, she supposed, when each season might bring work on a different ranch, and a person needed to be flexible enough about personalities to get things done.

She and Susanna wrestled the kitchen into order while the pile of flattened boxes in the garbage skip outside grew. The two of them made a little ceremony out of lighting the cooktop for the first time and turning on the oven to preheat.

"This is so exciting," Susanna said with a grin. "It actually works."

"Don't let Noah King hear you say that," Gideon said as he passed the door.

"I did hear that," their head carpenter called from upstairs. "Those propane lines passed inspection with flying colors."

"Maybe we should have gone ahead and put thicker insulation in," Susanna grumbled. "The soundproofing around here is terrible."

"We put in the thickest there was," Gideon reminded her. "If you don't talk behind people's backs, you won't have to worry about them overhearing you."

Susanna stuck out her tongue at him and got busy slicing potatoes, while he took his armload of flattened boxes outside with the smile of a man who has managed to get in the last word.

The last boxes in the keeping room contained their books. But in one labeled KEEPSAKES, Rachel found her engagement clock, one or two pictures, and the framed wedding sampler Grossmammi had stitched in the forties. Its wrapping, luckily, was one of the missing pillowcases for her bed. Such a beautiful piece of work—under a bouquet of cross-stitched roses were Grossmammi and Grossdaadi's names, their wedding date, and in a paler thread, like a quiet promise, she'd stitched the words of Ruth, peeping out from between the ribbons of the bouquet.

Whither thou goest, I will go
And where thou lodgest, I will lodge
Thy people shall be my people

And thy God my God

Words Ruth had lived by. Grossmammi had been no different, coming out to the Siksika Valley and leaving behind everything she'd known in Holmes County. And Rachel herself, settling in New Mexico, a state so different from Montana it might as well have been on another continent, going in faith with the man she loved.

"Your folks had that hanging in the front room," Luke said from behind her.

She controlled a start of surprise. Of all things for a man to remember. "They did. And now it's going here."

The river rock fireplace had a thick mantel made of a big, reddish chunk of wood that was likely from one of the Douglas firs felled to build this inn. She liked its solidity—and its plate groove—so instead of replacing it, she'd applied some sandpaper, some elbow grease, and some furniture polish to make it good as new. She stood the sampler in its frame in the groove, nodded with satisfaction, and set the clock beside it.

"We have to talk with the bishop about having church here," she said.

"Why wouldn't you?"

She gestured from the clock to the furniture. "This isn't a private home. We share it with guests. Imagine if you were an *Englisch* fisherman looking for his breakfast on a Sunday morning with all of us in here singing."

Luke's lips twitched, as if they couldn't quite remember how to smile. "*Gut* point. But how would you feel if your home wasn't open to *Gott*'s people?"

He had hit the nail on the head. "We're having a barn raising soon, apparently. Noah showed me some drawings that had a meeting room upstairs, next to the bunkhouse. It seems like a *gut* solution."

"You'll have an inn and a bunkhouse both?"

She explained her plan about boarding hired hands. "It's a compromise, I know, but at least the space would be meant for church from the beginning. This one never was. And if we get some Amish boys coming through as hands, well, it won't be a problem at all."

He nodded, surveying the keeping room. "Looks like you're about done."

"Just the books left," she agreed. "And then I think we're officially moved in."

"Let me do those," he said. "Do you like them organized by subject? Or by author?"

She gazed at him. "This isn't the public library."

He shrugged. "Makes them easier to find. I worked at one outfit where the lady of the house had them organized by color."

With a snort, she said, "Ours are probably organized by child. Go ahead and shelve them any way you want to. I've only ever moved twice, but I've found that over time, things migrate to where they're supposed to be anyway."

"Like people."

But his voice was so low as he pulled open the flaps of the box that she figured she wasn't meant to reply ... or even to hear.

He'd only been back in the Siksika a few hours. As curious as she was to hear his story, now was not the time. Maybe it never would be. Because along with how to cook and the habits of migrating belongings, she had learned that people's feelings and memories were their own, unless they chose otherwise.

Maybe it was best if she didn't know. After roundup in September, he'd probably move on, taking winter work in a feed store or heading to Texas, where the feed lots were. The younger wranglers often worked the ski hills or ice rinks, keeping body and soul together just until spring breakup, when the ice melted out of the rivers and the cycle of ranch work would begin again.

Supper was a cheerful meal, not only because of her Fiesta ware and the red checkered oilcloth on the table, but also because of savory beef stew over mashed potatoes, and heaps of golden biscuits running with butter. Susanna had filled the pantry with the canning from last year, so they had pickled beans and carrots, as well as a cabbage and beet pickle coleslaw.

Her hungry family did justice to the meal. Afterward, their guest leaned back in his chair and shook his head. "That is without a doubt the best meal I have enjoyed in a year. Maybe more."

Heat prickled in Rachel's cheeks. "*Denki*, Luke. The beef and the cabbage are from the Circle M. Naomi made certain we wouldn't go hungry until I could get out and buy some groceries."

"It takes a village to make a supper as good as this," Tobias agreed. "Or maybe I was just hungry."

"I was *starving*," little Gracie informed him. "Tomorrow can I have a cookie after school so I'm not so hungry?"

Rachel kept her lips firmly closed and let her eldest manage his children.

Except that he glanced at her with such appeal that all her good intentions melted away. "Of course you can," she said. "That is, if Aendi Susanna and I have time to make cookies."

"They'll have cookies at the Circle M," Benny said. "We can go there first."

"Malena makes the best chocolate chip," Gracie confided to Luke. "She's going to teach me how."

"Seems like you're old enough," Luke said solemnly.

"I'm *seven*. We both are," she amended, glancing at her brother. "But I came out first, so I'm the oldest."

"And the bossiest," mumbled her brother.

"Ben," their father said.

"Well, she is."

"But you'll be the tallest," Luke told him, by way of looking on the bright side. "If you keep eating meals like this." And then, as though he'd been swamped by a memory, his face lost its color. He pushed back his chair. "I'd best be on my way, or Hezekiah will lock me out."

He'd collected his coat and hat and was out the door before Rachel could do much more than snatch up her knitted shawl to follow him.

She closed the door behind her. The night was cold, but not nearly as cold as December. "Luke, wait! What do you want done with your things? And do you know where you're going?"

He was halfway to the gate, but he stopped, his shoulders hunching as though he'd realized he'd fled empty-handed. The parking lot was faintly illuminated by the street light at the feed store across the highway, but under the brim of his hat, she couldn't see much but his mouth, drawn tight against some emotion.

"Sorry," he managed. "If you have someplace I could leave the saddle, I'll just collect my duffel. And *ja*, I do remember the way. Though when I lived here, Creekside Lane was just a two-track."

She'd forgotten, but he was right. For their buggy's sake, she was glad it was paved now. "You can't see the creek path at night, and it's all mud anyway, but once the ground firms up, it's a nice walk. This property shares a back fence with Will and Zeke's land. Which I only found out during the sale. I look at it as a benefit, having my cousins so handy. With the Circle M five miles away, Reuben and Naomi couldn't help much if something went wrong."

They'd returned to the porch, so he bent and swung his duffel to his shoulder. "Where should I put the saddle?"

"Tobias will take it downstairs. There's a big cellar with a woodstove, a storage room that's too small, and a walk-in pantry that's just right. You'd think they knew we were coming when they built it."

After a moment, he said, "Nothing will go wrong, Rachel."

"I hope not. I believe *der Herr* brought us here and showed me the Inn for a reason. I'm stepping out in faith and hoping He'll also show us lots of fishermen and hunters."

"And tourists."

"And honeymooners and skiers." She huffed a laugh. "For a woman who never spoke to anyone but her own family and the hands from one month to the next, it will be a shock to my system to talk to a different bunch of strangers every day."

"I'm sure you can handle it. You used to be a pretty social person, if I remember right."

"Maybe. But we all change. You know as well as anyone that there are more big silences on a ranch than small talk."

"I never thought of it that way. I guess you mean out on the range."

"Well, hopefully not around the dinner table."

"No danger of that here." Then, as if he thought he might have offended her, he said, "I mean—"

"I know what you meant. We're a talkative bunch, but if you'd rather keep your peace when you're here, we won't insist on conversation."

He gave a slow shrug, as though the duffel wasn't sitting properly. "I've had a fair spell of keeping my peace. A little talk would probably be *gut* for me. *Guder nacht*, Rachel. Thanks again for supper—and for the work."

"You're welcome."

She stood in the shelter of the porch, pulling her shawl more tightly around her, and watched him cross the lot to the little bridge. He moved with the ease of someone used to walking or riding, except for a little extra weight on the right side that could have been to counterbalance the duffel, or the result of some old injury. There wasn't a rancher alive who hadn't been thrown—including herself and Susanna, during one particularly memorable roundup—so it might be that.

When she could no longer see him, she turned and went in, the warmth of the house gathering her in like an old friend. Susanna and Seth were doing the dishes, the twins settled at the family table with their spelling words, sent home yesterday because they'd missed school today. From upstairs came the syncopated rhythm of Tobias and Gideon's hammers. She'd check the twins' work in a minute. For now, she collected the Coleman lamp from the guest dining room and took it into the keeping room.

Boxes no longer cluttered the floor, and the carpet had been swept. The shelves running around the room to the height of the windowsills were about half full—the books not all crammed into one, but distributed among the bays in a way that invited more books, or maybe the placement of a keepsake or a vase of flowers.

So, cowboy, what order did you choose for our books? She set the lamp on the mantel and let her gaze run over the spines.

How about that.

It wasn't quite like a library, but enough so that it would feel familiar to a guest. Old favorites like the Little House books and Lucy Maud Montgomery's Anne books were shelved together. Her gardening and permaculture books filled an entire section. Even her cookbooks were here; she'd have to relocate them to the kitchen. All the children's books were in one place, and the fiction populated the shelves close to the window seat, as if anticipating the kind of reader who would appreciate curling up there.

The Luke she'd once known had not been a reader. He'd barely even been a scholar, more interested in his social life and in getting work on one of the ranches so he could save up for a saddle and a horse of his own. But evidently over the years he'd become familiar enough with libraries that he could make one here.

She'd have to thank him for it.

And try not to be too curious about what else might have changed so profoundly that she could no longer say she knew him.

≈ঽ   5   ঽ≈

Wednesday, April 27

"They'll be branding and giving shots on the Circle M today." Willard Zook forked up another mouthful of what he called *egg pie*, but which Luke considered the next thing to heaven. "Coming with us and Rachel's boys to lend a hand?"

He shook his head. "I'm hired to swing a hammer at the Inn until opening day. What is in this pie?"

"Eggs," Willard said.

"And goat cheese, some bacon, some herbs," Hezekiah said modestly. "Just what I had on hand."

"It's *wunderbaar*. I'll have another piece, and some potatoes, too."

It was five in the morning, and if he'd thought he'd have to make do with a bachelor's breakfast of baked beans heated on the stove in the can, he was wrong. Even the pastry was as good as any his wife had made, and Eva had been known for her pastry. Luke felt the familiar clutch in his gut at the thought of her, and swallowed hard to make the home-fried potatoes go down.

"I sure appreciate your giving me a bed," he said, digging into the second piece of pie. "It's comfortable. I can't give you anything for room and board until I'm paid, though. The bus fare took the last of what I had in my pocket."

Willard snorted, and Hezekiah looked downright offended. "As if we'd take money from a guest," the latter grumbled. "Particularly a guest who's an old friend."

"Can't be much of a friend if you haven't heard from him in thirty years," Luke pointed out wryly.

"Friends don't age like vegetables," Will said. "More like cheese. You could use a friend or two, and here we are."

That he could. "*Denki*, Will, Zeke. If I can do anything to help you out around here, I will."

"Oh, I have a feeling our cousin Rachel will give you plenty to do," Hezekiah said around his potatoes.

They gave him a lift to the Inn in the wagon, and after he'd jumped down, Gideon, Tobias, Seth and the twins clambered in.

"Bye, Luke, see you after school," Gracie called as the entourage clattered through the gate.

He lifted a hand in farewell, and when he turned toward the house, he was smiling.

Rachel turned in with him. "You came prepared, I see."

He'd unearthed his tool belt from the depths of the duffel, complete with hammer hanging from its leather loop, a leather bag of finishing nails, a measuring tape, a pocket-sized level, and a stud finder. "Figured I ought to do more than eat. Don't your sons have horses?"

"They're at the Circle M. Such a time we had getting them trailered out here. The first man I hired found something he liked better and took my money with him. Good thing we hadn't got the horses and tack loaded, or they'd have gone, too. The second outfit was more trustworthy—except they went to the Rocking Diamond by mistake. Reuben got that straightened out, and they were at the ranch waiting for us when we arrived."

"You'll be anxious for your barn raising."

She nodded, her hair concealed under her neat white *Kapp*. "Not long now. Until then, Reuben will take their keep out of his nephews' pay."

"So it's settled? They've hired on there for this year?" He didn't begrudge her sons a job, but it made one less place in the valley where he might find one, too.

"The younger ones have. I'm not sure about Tobias. He might want work closer to home, and have the twins go to school in this church district. Five miles is too much for them to walk in any season, never mind the winter." She glanced at him. "By the way, when was the last time you were able to go to church? In the Ventana Valley?"

"No, it was midweek when I got there, and the bishop and his family left Saturday. I don't even remember the time before that. After Christmas?" He tried to remember where they'd be by now in the preaching. Had New Life been coming up?

"Well, for us it's Council Meeting. Naomi tells me that both churches will go to the bishop's house, and then back on their regular Sunday for Communion." She paused. "If you plan to stay, you're just in time. I'm sure the *Ordnung* has seen some changes since we all lived here."

He expected it had. Outsiders thought the *Ordnung* was like the Ten Commandments, written in stone. But it was more like a living discipline, carried in the hearts and minds of the *Gmay*. Some things remained the same in a community, like the widths of hat brims, but others had the flexibility to change, like allowing the use of cell phones in far-flung, sometimes dangerous ranch country.

It had been a long time since he'd lived under the *Ordnung*. If he went to Council Meeting, it would say to the churches here that he meant to submit himself to it. But for how long? Luke didn't think he had it in him just now to answer that question. Getting here at all had been enough of an effort. And looking too far into the future, making plans, was dangerous.

Strange that he'd returned to the Siksika just in time for the holiest days of the Amish year. Or maybe not so strange. Jesus had been a carpenter, careful and observant of every detail. *Der Herr* clearly shared the same ability to pay minute attention even to a life as insignificant as his own.

"Speaking of change, sun's coming up," he said at last. "Where do you want me to start?"

"That's for Noah to say, while we still have him."

He followed her and the sound of hammering up the stairs, which had been refinished and had a paper runner tacked down to protect them from the workmen's boots. The floors on the upper level were newly laid but unvarnished, the planks looking raw but still giving hints of warm color. They found Noah King in the suite at the far end, nailing sheathing over the bats of insulation between the studs.

"I thought you'd be at the Circle M for branding," Luke said to the young man. "Don't you live there?"

"*Ja*, but they have lots of hands and Rachel only has you and me. At least through Saturday." He quirked an eyebrow at their employer.

"You won the bid you were hoping for?" Rachel asked, looking almost happy for him.

"We did." He grinned, and the square, solemn lines of his face warmed under the four months' growth of a married man's beard. "The folks who bought that old house on Pumphouse Road want it taken back to the studs and renovated. Along with this job, it'll be a nice start to Rebecca's and my savings account."

Rachel looked as though she wanted to say something, then changed her mind. "I'm happy for you. Truly. Well, I'll leave you two here. Today has to be grocery day or we'll all be on an enforced diet. Can Susanna and I borrow Hester and the buggy, Noah?"

Luke had seen the lone buggy horse grazing in a makeshift paddock on the lawn.

"Of course."

Luke soon found the familiar rhythm in banging nails and hanging 'rock. Every nail was a thank-you to Rachel for giving him work, for bringing his old friends back into his life—even for this young man, Noah King. His attitude was one Luke hadn't seen in a long time. They even got to talking about it after a while.

"Carpentry is more than a job to me," Noah explained as they hung the final panel of Sheetrock and secured it with the battery-operated screw gun. "Building homes for people is like building the future, isn't it? This room, for instance. It's not just four walls, windows, and a door. It's where some city people, maybe, will find a refuge and some quiet. Or a young couple just married will find what a difference bringing each other a cup of *Kaffee* can make to a day. And most of all—" He stood back to run a critical eye over the seam. "Every nail brings my wife and I closer to a home of our own."

"You plan to build, not buy?" Luke had never owned his own home. He and Eva could never afford to do much more than rent. And then ... afterward ... home was the last place he wanted to be. Deserved to be.

"It's what I do," Noah said cheerfully. "Let's get these seams taped, and I'll stir up some mud. It'll dry by tonight and we can finish all the painting in the morning."

At midday, Rachel had come back with bags of groceries and made more biscuits to go with last night's leftover stew. Noah delivered a tub of chocolate chip cookies compliments of Malena, his sister-in-law.

"It's a constant picnic around here," Rachel said with a laugh as she and Susanna took the dishes to the sink afterward. "But things ought to settle down now with the refrigerator and the pantry both full. I'm looking forward to getting out my favorite recipes again."

"It all tasted great to me," Luke said as he and Noah headed back upstairs. "*Denki*, Rachel."

"I think you've put on a whole pound since yesterday," she called after him.

He had no business getting warm in the face at the thought that she'd been inspecting his old bones. But as he and Noah painted the next day, it became clear that Rachel was honestly interested in whether he was healthy or not. It had been a long time since he'd heard more than a curt demand from a ranch foreman about whether he was able to ride. It was also why he felt he ought to put in extra hours in the evening. And though they had to have been exhausted from roping and wrestling calves all day, Rachel's sons pitched in.

With all the walls painted the warm cream that Rachel had chosen, on Friday Noah got them started painting the bedroom doors and what seemed like miles of baseboard trim the same color. "Some people like every room a different color," Rachel said as she worked, steadily painting the doors laid across sawhorses. "The thought of buying a dozen little cans of paint to do that gives me hives."

"And the volume discount from the Yoders is nice," Noah added cheerfully.

"They have *everything* over there," Susanna said. "Whether I need *Kapp* strings or a new hymnbook or a Coleman lamp or a twenty-pound bag of flour, they have it."

On Saturday, Noah's last day with them, Luke and Tobias and the two Miller women watched closely as Noah demonstrated how to measure and cut the window trim and crown molding, and how to put up the latter so that the pieces butted together at an angle in the corners for that handmade antique look.

They'd managed to get two rooms completed by the time the sun was sinking behind the pines. Noah dusted off his hands and leaned in to talk to Rachel and Susanna, who were working in the big room closest to the stairs.

"I won't stay for supper, Rachel. They'll be expecting me at the Circle M, and we tend to have a quiet evening before church. Especially tomorrow. It will be a big day."

"All right. We'll stop now, too. Don't forget to send me your invoice."

Luke ambled down the hall to say good-bye, and thanked Noah for teaching him a thing or two more about carpentry. The fine points of finish work had never been part of a job he'd worked on before.

"We'll see you tomorrow at Little Joe's?" Noah asked.

"You will." He hadn't quite got over the news at dinner the other night that Little Joe Wengerd was now the bishop in this district. He'd been even more of a rule-breaker than Luke had, and that was saying something. "Will and Zeke won't mind me tagging along."

As far as working out his salvation went, there had been some pretty dry days on ranches owned by *Englisch* folk, when there wasn't an Amish settlement within a day's bus ride. Dry spells weren't good for the spirit. When a man had as little as Luke did, fellowship with others in the church was like a spring, feeding and softening the ground of his soul. Even if he had to submit to the local *Ordnung*, it was worth it.

"Noah, maybe I'll follow your example and head over to Will and Zeke's a little early."

"Want a ride?" Noah was packing up his tools. "I'll be ready in a minute."

"It's out of your way," Luke protested.

"Actually, Noah," Rachel said, as though an idea had just occurred to her, "maybe you could give both of us a ride. I have a matter to discuss with my cousins. Susanna, there's chicken to bake for dinner, and take your pick of the vegetables. Seth, if you want scalloped potatoes, you'll need to help your sister and peel and slice them. I'll be back by six o'clock."

"What are you going to discuss now that you can't tomorrow after church?" Susanna asked blankly.

"Tomorrow is sacred to its purpose," he mother informed her. "While you pack up, I'll get Hester hitched."

One thing about Rachel—she had a gift for organizing people. Luke barely had time to clean up and get his own tools ready to resume work on Monday when he heard the clatter of Hester's hooves in the parking lot as Rachel backed her between the slats of Noah's buggy.

He couldn't imagine what she needed to talk over with Will and Zeke so suddenly, but it wasn't his business, either. He didn't have much to say on the way over, sitting in the back of the buggy to give Rachel the seat next to Noah. Noah dropped them off, and with a cheery wave, set off

THE AMISH COWBOY'S REFUGE

down County Road 37, which, if Luke remembered right, went past the old Fischer place and curved back around to the highway at a bridge within walking distance of the Circle M's lane.

He followed Rachel into the house, where Willard and his brother were in the kitchen, just beginning preparations for dinner.

"Rachel," Will said in surprise. "Are you returning your carpenter because he doesn't work?"

She obviously hadn't forgotten her cousin's sense of humor in her years away. With a grin, she said, "On the contrary, he's worth every cent of the money I haven't paid him yet."

"I don't know about that," Luke said, shucking off his coat and hanging it on a hook in the mud room. He took her coat, still warm from her body and smelling faintly like a lavender field in June.

Which was not what he should be thinking of the woman who signed his paycheck. The woman who had been his best friend's wife.

"Are you staying for dinner, Rachel?" Hezekiah asked. "I can set another plate."

"*Neh, denki.* I told Will here that I wanted to take up a matter with the two of you. Noah King said something today that made me think I shouldn't waste any time finding out what you both think."

Willard took the coffee pot from the stove and filled it at the sink for a fresh brew. "About that parcel?"

"*Ja.* Did you get around to telling Hezekiah what I want to do?"

The Zook brothers had talked it over at breakfast one day in front of Luke, but he'd had to leave for work before they'd come to any conclusions.

"We had some discussion," Willard allowed. "Are you still set on it?"

"I think it's a *gut* idea. Noah's whole goal is to earn enough to make a home for my niece. He's certainly gone above and beyond to make a home for us, so I have no doubt he'll achieve it. But think of the years he could shave off his labors if I deeded that property to him."

"That's very generous, Rachel," Luke managed. Imagine having enough money and land that you could just give portions of it away.

"It isn't—not really," she said. "That five-acre piece is in a funny location. It's a bit of a dogleg, a pain in the neck to keep fenced, and no good at all to grow hay unless I planned to seed the Inn's entire property. Which I don't." She flicked a glance between her cousins. "You two are welcome to lease everything for hay but the lots the Inn and its future barn stand on, if you want to."

Willard's brows went up as he looked over his shoulder at them from the stove. "We'd be interested, for sure and certain."

"But it's not such a funny piece of dirt if all you plan is a house, a barn, and a shop," Hezekiah mused, putting the cream and sugar on the table as Willard brought the coffee over and poured four mugs. "Even has a little creek frontage, if you don't mind those big granite rocks."

"Noah probably doesn't care about rocks," she pointed out. "But I won't go ahead and offer it to him in lieu of pay unless you think it's a *gut* idea. You'd be their closest neighbors, after all."

"More of a problem for them than us," Hezekiah said modestly. "Hope young *Fraa* King doesn't mind goats."

"Probably not—until she puts her garden in," Rachel said.

Hezekiah glanced at his brother. "Guess we'd better give that fence some attention after all."

"Guess so."

"So it's settled, then." Rachel took a sip of her coffee. Luke observed that she still took it creamy, no sugar. He was the opposite—black, and lots of sugar.

"When are you going to tell him?" Willard asked. "If it's in lieu of pay, it seems to me it had best be soon."

She nodded. "He's supposed to bring me his invoice next week. Poor boy, he hasn't been paid since he started in February. And he's turned that inn from a falling-down wreck into something that's practically new."

"Rachel," Luke blurted, then felt the heat in his cheeks. "Sorry. None of my business. It just seems—"

"I know. I told him to track all his hours, but even without that, I can multiply two and a half months by twelve-hour days. He's earned that funny piece of land, no doubt about it. I just hope my niece isn't too angry with me for keeping him away from the Circle M all this time."

Luke had a feeling that even if she was, the sheer love and respect for her young husband that lay behind Rachel's gift would smooth the way to forgiveness.

೫ 6 ೫

Sunday, May 1

LITTLE JOE WENGERD STARED at Luke as though he were a ghost. "Bless me," he said at last. "Luke Hertzler, as I live and breathe."

It had been a good many years since Luke had been to Council Meeting here at the Wengerd place, but some things never changed. The married men still congregated in front of the barn doors before the service, and the single ones would no doubt still be the last to find their seats. He remembered a time or two when he and Little Joe had to be hunted up and chivvied into church, flicking their cigarettes into the garden behind the older men's backs, and hoping Fraa Wengerd didn't find the butts until days later.

Luckily he'd had the sense to quit smoking not long after that. Maybe Little Joe had, too.

"It's good to see you, Bishop." Luke couldn't quite keep his lips from twitching.

"The Lord works in mysterious ways," Joe replied easily.

Those two sentences contained an entire conversation about the unlikelihood of a rapscallion being chosen by *Gott* to serve and minister to His church. But in the end, if a man had been baptized and committed himself to the Amish way of worship, he had to be willing to go the distance, to tie himself upon the altar of sacrifice. And for an Amish man, finding the short piece of straw in the *Ausbund* meant the full extent of that sacrifice.

Joe, the minister, and the two preachers left them shortly after that, to find a quiet room in which to prepare themselves for the morning ahead. And soon Luke found himself sitting in church once again with Willard and Hezekiah, as though the years had somehow telescoped together. As single men, but around the age of fifty, it was not seemly for them to sit with the *Youngie* any more. And with Luke being a widower, and their guest, nothing could be more natural than for him to join them. To prevent himself from looking across at the women's side, he studied the men around him. There was Josiah Keim, looking as ropy and strong as most ranchers did, his hair much more gray than Luke's own. And there was Paul Petersheim, who apparently ran a butcher shop where most of the Amish took their meat for processing and freezing. Last, Luke recognized Abram Yoder, owner of Yoder's Variety Store, who had married Della Steiner and produced a string of children.

So few left in the valley of the gang he had run around with!

But, he supposed, people found partners and moved on to where land was obtainable and a life could be made. The Siksika and its mountain slopes favored ranching; those with a hankering to push their hands into the soil would not find it very hospitable. Not with a three-month growing season. His own parents had given up trying, which was why, a year or so after Marlon and Rachel's wedding, they had returned to Wisconsin. And he'd seen no way out other than to go with them.

On the dot of eight, as the single men were straggling in and making more noise than they should, the *Vorsinger* began the first hymn. And on the second verse of the *Loblied*, the elders came in and took their seats before the joint congregation.

How wise Little Joe was in this innovation. After the sermon, the unbaptized were released while church members from both districts remained to hear his instruction of the *Ordnung*, be informed of changes simultaneously, and all be encouraged together. But, Luke supposed, the *Gmay* here in the Siksika still all fit into the bishop's home, and it was a *gut* opportunity to reinforce the ties that bound them. From the numbers of *Youngie* and *Kinner*, not many years would pass before Little Joe would be forced to move his joint congregation into a barn or shop.

There was comfort in a Council Meeting's unchanging rhythms. And, since it had been so long for him, Luke even found a kind of comfort in the fact that he would have to pay a visit to Yoder's Variety Store and get himself a Siksika style felt hat and a pair of suspenders the correct width if he wanted to fit in with the *Ordnung* here.

Ah well. It was time for a new hat, anyway. His old one had definitely seen better days and more than one errant hoof.

After a prayer and a final hymn, it was time for the fellowship meal. While the young men got to work setting up tables, he ambled outside. The sun had chosen a *gut* day to shine, and the air had that freshly washed feeling of leaves greening the trees while the daffodils in the bed against the house lifted their delicate heads.

With the joint congregation, it was too much to expect that the bishop's household should provide all the food. So each family had brought something to contribute. Willard and Hezekiah had prepared a basket that no one in his right mind would complain about—turnovers filled with baked cheese and olives and peppers. The Millers on the Circle M had brought sliced roast beef sandwiches slathered with horseradish so hot Luke's eyes watered. Of course there was the usual *bohnesuppe*, sandwiches thick with peanut butter spread, and pies and cookies galore. They washed their lunch down with freshly brewed coffee.

When he thanked Will and Zeke for including him, half of him wanted to stay close by them, like an old steer seeking the protection of younger animals. Not that they were any younger, but at least he'd have someone to watch his back if the questions got too piercing. Luke fortified himself with a final gulp of coffee, and headed outside once again, making his diffident way among knots of people.

Josiah Keim stared at him for a full, agonizing second of complete non-recognition when Luke walked up and offered his hand. Then the identity of this stranger standing there so awkwardly seemed to click in his brain. "Luke?" he said in disbelief. "Is it really you, after all this time?" He seized Luke's hand in the lifelong rancher's iron grip. "Kathryn," he said to the woman next to him, "it's Luke Hertzler."

The rounded, red-cheeked woman's wide eyes filled with warmth. "Welcome back to the valley, Luke," she said. "Remember me?"

It took another second for her smile to find its past owner in his memory. "Kathryn Steiner? You stayed in the valley, too?"

"I wasn't going to, but this one here changed my mind."

She turned the smile on her husband. "Have you met our daughter Sylvia? She's still at home with us. We had eight, you know. All the others are married—our two older sons working the ranch with Josiah, four girls in other communities in Montana, and our youngest son in Colorado."

The river of happy facts flowed past him as he nodded at Sylvia Keim, who appeared to be somewhere north of twenty-five. She was blond, as Josiah had been back in their single days, and she had the stooped look of a tall woman trying not to be noticed. Her face was full of kindness, and even from here, her gaze followed the herd of *Kinner* running from pasture fence to kitchen door to creek, watching in case someone fell down ... or fell in.

"Are you here with your family for a visit?" Sylvia asked shyly, returning her gaze to him.

And just like that, in a few gentle words, his worst fear was forced out in the open.

"Oh—" Kathryn said on a kind of gasp. "Sylvia, look, Tobias Miller's twins are heading down to the creek. Better stop them before they get themselves soaked—they won't know where the undercuts are."

"But Mamm, Tobias is—"

"He's talking to his cousin Daniel. Hurry, now."

When the younger woman obeyed, despite the fact that Tobias was close by, the color in Kathryn's cheeks had spread across her whole face.

"Sorry about that, Luke," Josiah said. "She didn't know."

"No harm done," he managed. "It comes up once in a while."

"How many years has it been?" Kathryn asked gently.

"We'd been married ten, so ..." He made the effort to think, though for years his brain had shied away from doing just that, like a horse spotting a rattler in the trail. "Seventeen, maybe?"

Seventeen years since that night. It didn't seem possible. Maybe because totalling up the years would show how long he'd been on the run from the memories.

"And you've never..." Kathryn's voice trailed away.

"Maybe he doesn't want to go over all that, *Fraa*," Josiah said, watching him. "Especially not five minutes after shaking hands."

Luke pulled himself together. These had been his friends, once. There was no reason to think they weren't still. "It's all right. *Neh*, I've never wanted to court again. Too busy keeping body and soul together."

"Cowboying?" Josiah smiled. "It's what we knew, back then."

He nodded. "It's in my blood, probably the way it is in yours. I've been all over—everywhere west of Wisconsin that grazed beef. And finally I wound up at this outfit in New Mexico and heard there was an Amish *Gmay* over Ventana Valley way. Turns out it was where Marlon and Rachel had settled."

"You were *Neuwesitzer* at their wedding, weren't you?" Kathryn had recovered from her embarrassment. "I remember that day well. Kept hoping it would give Josiah here ideas."

"That it did," her husband said comfortably. "I think I proposed not long after."

"You think." She batted him on the arm. "I like that."

Luke couldn't help but smile at their companionable humor. "Looks like it was a wise choice," he said. "If I remember, Josiah, you were as silent as a fence post most of the time. I suppose Kathryn balanced you out."

"He was not silent," Kathryn protested. "We used to talk long into the night. Still do, on occasion."

"I guess it depends on the company," Josiah admitted. "So what are your plans?"

"I'm banging nails over at Rachel's inn for the time being."

His old friend cocked an eyebrow. "Didn't you just tell me you were cowboying?"

"I picked up a skill or two over the years. Winters, you know. You have to do something."

"There's hardly an Amishman alive who doesn't know what to do with a hammer," Kathryn pointed out. "Are you staying there too?"

This woman had no fear of speaking up. No wonder Josiah had learned to converse. "*Neh*, they've only just moved in themselves. I'm bunking with her cousins. Willard and Hezekiah Zook."

"Ah, I remember the connection now," Kathryn said. "How is the renovation coming? I have to say, it was a nine days' wonder around here when she bought that old wreck of a place. After all those years of ranching!"

"We're all getting on, Kate," her husband reminded her. "She's got her boys, but a woman running a ranch alone ..." He trailed off, then added, "And ranches don't grow on trees. Only one has come up for sale around here in the last two years." He met Luke's gaze. "We're all afraid some *Englisch* developer will buy the next one and put condos on it instead of cattle."

"Let's hope not," Kathryn said with a shudder. "Luke, maybe you'll come to us for dinner some night?"

How strange it felt to be invited out for a meal. Other than Rachel and the Zook brothers, the last time had been the bishop in New Mexico, and it had been a pick-up affair since they were leaving the day after he did.

"I'd like that," he said. "But I'd best put it off until after the rivers open. I'm working long hours to get the renovation done, and then there's all the floors to be finished before the guest furniture is delivered and set up. It's going to be tight as it is."

"What do the rivers have to do with anything?" Josiah said, puzzled.

"Rachel wants to cast a line for a few fishermen, so she's opening the day before. Say, you don't know any *Englisch* who might make her one of those ..." He thought for a moment. "A web? *Neh*, that ain't it."

A young woman in a lavender dress with matching cape and apron was passing just in time to hear. She stopped. "A website?"

He nodded to her. "That's the word. I knew it had something to do with spiders."

"Luke Hertzler, this is Julie Stolzfus," Kathryn said. "Her mother is Rose, who owns Rose Garden Quilts."

The girl's eyes sparkled with interest. "Are you the cowboy helping Rachel Miller at the Inn?" When he nodded, she went on, "We live in town, maybe a block away on the far side of the bridge. *Mei Bruder* is the blacksmith and farrier. And *ja*, I do know someone who could make a website for her. One of the girls on the hockey team does it for a living."

Luke couldn't imagine making a living out of something that didn't actually exist in the physical world, but he couldn't fault anything that kept a roof over one's head. "You might bring her over some night to meet Rachel, and she can tell her what she needs."

"I'll do that." Julie looked pleased at being able to help. "This week."

"If that wasn't *der Herr* leading that *Maedscher* past us just at the right moment, I don't know what was," Kathryn said comfortably. "Her brother Alden is courting Rachel's niece Malena, you know."

"I didn't," he admitted. "I fell off the Amish grapevine some years ago."

Josiah snorted. "Give it time," he said. Then he gripped Luke's shoulder briefly. "*Kumm*. Paul Petersheim is over there by the fence with his sons, looking like he's seen a ghost. Better go over and reassure him you're real."

And with a smile at Kathryn, he allowed himself to be led away to resurrect the friendships of the past. Without, he hoped, any reference to the mistakes that still lay in hiding there.

❧

RACHEL AND NAOMI STOOD ON THE BISHOP'S WIDE, welcoming covered porch, watching people visiting, their groups forming and reforming as people came and went in the spring sunshine.

"I like this idea of a joint Council Meeting," Rachel said.

"It's not often we're able to have fellowship like this with the other congregation," Naomi agreed.

As bishop, Little Joe Wengerd oversaw the flock in the western district one Sunday, then the eastern part of the valley, including part of the town of Mountain Home, the next. At the rate the *Gmay* was growing, Rachel mused, by the time her *Kinner* were all married, they might have to split the congregation again and *Gott* would need another bishop. But that was all in His hands. Goodness knew she had enough to fill her own.

"He began it not long after he was ordained," Naomi said.

"Mind you, the *Gmay* was much smaller then. It took a while for the church to really establish itself here—the earliest families came in the seventies, and only Aendi Annie King is still here of that first group. Many leave. It's one thing to be familiar with raising cattle. It's another to do it in Montana during the winter."

"Separates the wheat from ... the barley, I suppose," Rachel agreed. "Is that Paul Petersheim Luke is talking to now? Goodness me, I haven't seen him ... well, since Marlon and I were newlyweds, I guess."

"He has the butcher shop in town," Naomi said. "And a freezer shed where we keep our meat and fish. You should see me at roundup, bringing home the meat for the elk stew. It's like having the weight of a whole other person in the buggy, wrapped in neat white packages."

"I'll need to go see him, then." Rachel made a mental note to herself. "To open an account."

"And here we are, talking business on the Lord's day," Naomi chided with a smile. "You go on. I can hear Deborah fussing inside. Now that I've had my lunch, it's time for hers. I know I should wean her, but I can't quite bring myself to do it yet."

Rachel wasn't normally shy in crowds, but it had been many years since she'd been in church with so many. The Ventana Valley *Gmay* had been small to begin with, and as families had begun moving away, it had reached the point where even their bishop had to admit the *Gmay* was too small to supply preachers and a minister, so he had reconciled himself to moving, too.

Susanna joined her as she went down the steps. "Why aren't you with the *Youngie*?" Rachel asked her. "It's not like you not to be in on all the doings."

"In this crowd, it's hard to know where to find the doings," her daughter said with a laugh. "The boys are over by the barn, Tobias is chasing the twins, and I'm ..." Her voice trailed off. "How are you making out, Mamm?"

"Oh, I'm fine. Just taking a breath before I plunge into Old Home Week. Naomi was pointing out some of the ones your *dat* and I used to know. Like Kathryn Steiner." She nodded in her direction. "Looks like she married Josiah Keim—which I predicted. Kathryn was crazy about him."

"Still is, looks like," Susanna said with a smile. "They're like you and Dat used to be."

Rachel eyed her. "And how was that?"

Susanna shrugged. "You know. Companionable. Easy together. Dat liked to laugh, and so did you."

True enough. Until the cancer had made it impossible to laugh, both because it pained him, and because he had worried about her and the ranch so much, toward the end.

Susanna's gaze had moved to the Petersheim group, which was looking very sober as Luke said something, his head bent. They weren't asking questions about what had happened to his family, were they? Surely old friends wouldn't be that insensitive? Not that she knew any more than anybody else. But neither did she want to see that bow in Luke's shoulders, as though he were protecting an old wound.

"It'll be *gut* for Luke to get to know people again," Susanna said, her gaze still on him. "When the work is completed at the Inn, he'll want to find work. Ranch work."

A frown flickered on Rachel's brow. "I suppose. But don't hurry him off too soon, *Dochsder*. We're not finished yet."

"Oh, I'm not. And I'm sure Willard and Hezekiah aren't, either. Do you think he'll stay in the Siksika?"

"No idea," Rachel said. "I thought you liked Luke."

Susanna looked at her in surprise. "I do. I like how hard he works, and how far we've come in just the few days he and Noah got to work together. But I—" She stopped, and a wave of color passed over her cheeks.

Rachel turned to face her fully, leaning one hip on the porch rail. "What, *Liewi?*"

"Don't be mad. I'm probably imagining things."

Now Rachel's mind was working overtime, imagining every sort of disaster. "I won't be mad," she managed. And if she was, she'd hold it in until Susanna had gone.

"I'm not sure it's altogether *gut* for Luke to be around outside of work," Susanna said at last.

It took a few seconds for Rachel to work through her meaning, and not like it one bit. "Why not? He is our *Bruder* in the *Gmay*. And he has no family. It's natural for a lonely man to want to be with people he knows."

"I know, but ... I'm just not sure I like the way he looks at you sometimes."

Rachel drew a breath into lungs that seemed to have constricted. "He looks at me as a *Schweschder*. The way he's always done."

"He's a widower. And you're a widow."

Rachel stared at her daughter, as deeply shocked as if Susanna had struck her. Because her guilty conscience had dealt her a slap every bit as hard.

"Maybe he's here for more than just work, is all," Susanna mumbled, her face flaming as she stared down into the daffodils below.

"I think you'd better find something more productive to fill that head with," Rachel finally managed. "You're doing an injustice to Luke, and you're being deeply disrespectful to me."

Susanna's lips trembled. "I'm sorry, Mamm. But you asked me."

"And I'm sorry I did. I hope you haven't shared this nonsense with anyone else."

"Neh." Her daughter was nearly in tears now.

"Gut." Rachel pulled a tissue out of her sleeve and handed it to her. "Here. Blow your nose. Kathryn Keim just waved at us. If that's her daughter in the raspberry colored dress, maybe you'd like to meet her."

Under the sheltering tissue, Susanna made a noise that sounded like, "Okay," and Rachel marched down the steps.

Not for worlds would she admit that as she did so, her knees were shaking. Because the last thing she wanted to admit was that Susanna—observant, thoughtful, emotional Susanna—might be right.

♔ 7 ♕

SUSANNA AND SYLVIA KEIM did not, Rachel was disappointed to see, hit it off right away. Maybe it was because Susanna was still upset. Maybe it was the age difference between the two. Whatever it was, Susanna offered a smile and drifted away toward her cousins, who were part of a circle of *Youngie* down by the creek.

Sylvia smiled at Rachel, then ducked her head and walked toward a grove of trees in the back forty, where a bunch of little girls seemed to be hunting for crocuses.

"She's a born mother, that one," Rachel said to Kathryn Keim. "But I seem to remember you shepherding your share of *Kinner* when we were that age, too."

"She comes by it honestly," Kathryn admitted, her fond gaze following her daughter. Then she sighed. "I'd sure like to wake up a few of the young men around here. She'd make such a good *Fraa*. Her mothering years are being wasted."

"*Gott* doesn't believe in waste," she said. "Everything He creates has its purpose."

"Ach, you're right." Kathryn shook her head. "I remember your Mamm saying that very thing."

"Probably when I was complaining about taking the scraps out to the chickens."

"Maybe so. How it comes back to me, with you here again. I've missed you, Rachel. The occasional letter and *Grischdaag* card just aren't the same."

"I've missed you, too. I wonder if Little Joe will put us in the eastern *Gmay* now that we've moved? We'd see each other quite often, then."

"Why don't you ask him yourself?" And before Rachel could say a word, Kathryn had flagged down the bishop and beckoned him over.

"Rachel," he boomed. "Are you all settled at the Inn?"

"Almost. It's feeling more like home, with our rugs and books around us again. I hope you and Sadie will come for dinner some night soon."

"How about tomorrow?"

Had he been waiting for the invitation, or had he decided to ask on the spot? Goodness. How different he was from their bishop in the Ventana country, who could take a week to decide on the same question. And what a good thing she'd got in the groceries.

"We'll look forward to it," she said. "I was just wondering out loud to Kathryn which district you'll be putting us in. Maybe we can talk that over tomorrow, too."

"No need." His bright blue gaze looked out over the pastures and rooftops in the distance, as though he could see the five miles to Mountain Home. "Seems it would be best for Tobias's young scholars and for you to be in the eastern district, *nix*? The schoolhouse is near the Zook brothers' place, down 37 not a quarter mile to the east, so they'd be handy to family if they needed them. That sound all right?"

Kathryn gripped her arm in delight, no doubt as happy as Rachel that they would be in church together. She wouldn't see the Circle M family every other Sunday, mind you, but there was no law that said she couldn't go to church in the other district if she wanted to—and no gate across the county highway preventing lots of visits, either.

"*Ja*, that sounds *wunderbaar*," she told him. "I hear a rumor there's to be a barn-raising June first. Soon there will be another place for the *Gmay* to meet."

"Best have young Noah King check that with the county planning department. You've got a heritage property, and there used to be a barn, if you remember. It might still be on the plot plan. That'll save you a bit on permit fees."

Rachel made a mental note to drop by the Circle M sooner rather than later to ask him. Maybe that would make a *gut* pretext by which to begin a conversation about that L-shaped lot, too.

"Zeke and Willard tell me Luke Hertzler is staying with them while he works at your place. And that you plan to put a bunkhouse in that barn and rent it out to hired hands."

"*Ja*, I do. *Englisch* guest or Amish hand, bed and board is the same amount of work to me," Rachel said. To reassure him, she added, "A big room for the *Gmay* to meet in would be next to it, upstairs—and if the hands have difficulty with that, they'll have to move on."

He laughed. "I guess they will. What about Luke?"

She met his gaze, puzzled. "What about him?"

"Is he going to be one of your boarders?"

She felt a little at sea with the swerve in topic. "I couldn't say. He doesn't share his future plans with us. You'd do better asking Willard."

"I did. He said Luke was welcome to board at their place, provided the goats made up their minds about him."

Kathryn giggled, and Rachel had to smile, too. Such a Willard thing to say. "I'm not entirely certain he ought to trust the opinion of a goat, Bishop."

He glanced around, as though they might have been overheard. "Keep your voice down with that kind of reckless talk. He's just over there, with Reuben and your boy Tobias." His eyes twinkling, he went on, "I'll look forward to seeing what you've done with that old wreck of a place tomorrow, Rachel. A *gut* reminder of what *der Herr* can do with a human soul, *nix?*"

Was it her imagination, or did his gaze stray toward Luke?

He strolled off—a six-foot-five man covered a lot of ground that way—and Kathryn moved a little closer. "I wonder why he was asking about Luke? The poor man has only just come back, and probably hasn't even got his bearings yet."

Rachel shook her head to indicate she didn't know, either. But in her memory, Susanna said, *I don't like the way he looks at you*, and Willard said, *It isn't fitting, a lone wrangler staying in the house here with you.*

What did they think was going to happen? That they'd fall into a mad, passionate embrace at their age?

It had happened plenty of times back in those long-ago days she was doing her best to forget. She hoped Luke had forgotten, too. He must have—in all the time he'd spent in the house, he'd never let slip by word or gesture that they had once been more than just friends. She had to be careful to follow his *gut* example.

Kathryn walked companionably beside Rachel as they

moved from group to group, making introductions when necessary and pointing out the remaining few who had known her family years ago. They had stopped to watch Sylvia, who was now doing her best to keep the little boys out of the creek —Benny included—when Kathryn said, "I suppose one of the advantages to being new to our *Gmay* here is that you won't have had time to offend anyone before Communion Sunday. If you were in the west district, you'd have to get it all settled quickly—their Sunday is next week."

"I'm ashamed to admit that with everything going on, I haven't had a moment to search my heart. I guess I'd better spend some time on my knees."

One of the most important requirements before taking part in Communion Sunday was that the heart must be cleansed of all ill-will, and forgiveness asked if you had committed an offense against another or even just hurt them by a careless word. Rachel had heard of terrible consequences for not asking forgiveness—the worst being communion put off until the dispute had been resolved and each party reconciled once more. Unwillingness and pride in one heart could affect the entire *Gmay*, which was why it was so important, twice a year, to cleanse the conscience before taking Christ's body and blood during the communion service.

Kathryn nudged her. "Remember the time your cousin Maryanna made a dress of a raspberry so close to red that you said something to her?"

Rachel groaned. "Do I. My goodness, she was so offended —and I could never understand why. I can't think of an Amish woman in three states who would wear red and have people reminded of the scarlet woman of Babylon every time they saw her."

"She loved that dress—to this day I remember all the little

pleats around the hems of the sleeves. The work it must have meant. And then her mother forbade her to wear it when it was finished."

"Adding coals to the fire," Rachel agreed. "It took me quite a while to get to the place where I could ask her to forgive me. Right up until the Saturday before, it was on my conscience. And then she looked all surprised and told me she'd cut it up for a quilt."

"But did she forgive you?"

"*Ja*, though she made it sound as if it wasn't necessary. It was to me, though."

Rachel could still remember how heavy the burden of guilt had been before she was able to say the words. It was worth it to ask Maryanna's forgiveness just to have that burden lifted.

She gazed at Zach Miller and Ruby Wengerd as they stood talking with Noah and Rebecca King, not really seeing them, her mind running over the past weeks and looking for something that needed to be put right. In the Ventana Valley? The one Amish rancher who had once expressed interest in the Four Winds had moved away with his family long ago, so her selling it to a worldly man couldn't offend him. She and the bishop had parted ways with handshakes and warm wishes. Her own children? *Neh*, she couldn't think of anything so serious that it needed to be cleared away—just those few odd words of Susanna's.

I don't like the way he looks at you.

Which would be a matter between them if Rachel had looked back at him in the same way. But since she hadn't noticed him looking at her in any way but in friendship or in polite attention as she gave him instructions, it was no matter at all.

"I can't think of anything serious enough to go to someone

and ask forgiveness for," she said to Kathryn at last. "But maybe I'd better talk it over with Tobias. The twins are old enough now to ask forgiveness of any of us for disobedience."

"And of each other for any of the thousand little things *Kinner* can get on each other's nerves about," Kathryn said. "I do that with my grandchildren, too. It's never too early to start saying you're sorry, as we all know."

It was after three o'clock, and while many seemed reluctant to leave, the spring light had faded as the sun sank into the tops of the pines. In a moment, they heard the jingle of harness as first one buggy and then another rolled down the lane.

Kathryn walked off toward Sylvia, presumably to convince her to come along so that they could head home. Rachel turned to see Luke in conversation with Willard and Zeke. Before she could find someone else to talk to, he had looked up and met her gaze. Then he walked over.

She had one second to be thankful that Susanna was nowhere in sight before he reached her. Then she castigated herself. Why shouldn't her carpenter and old friend come up and speak to her?

"Your cousins wondered if the family would like to join them for supper," Luke said.

"Them? Aren't you invited, too?"

"I am, but I'm not the men of the house." His lips quirked up in a smile. "Sounds funny to say it that way, doesn't it?"

"Seems funny that in all this time, neither of them ever found a woman who would put up with them," Rachel said with some affection. Even as boys, her cousins had been different. More interested in animals and plants than in people. She'd always thought it would have taken an extraordinary woman to get the attention of either one.

"I understand the general feeling is that if a woman accepted one, she'd have to settle for the other underfoot as well," Luke said. "Don't know if that's true, though. Doesn't seem sensible."

"One day maybe we'll find out," she said. "But for now, you can tell them we'd be very happy to come for supper. Those of us who aren't staying for the singing, that is. Seems a shame to let this day end, doesn't it?"

"It's been ... different," he said, but by way of agreement or not, she couldn't tell.

In the end, Tobias and the twins came in the buggy with Rachel, but Susanna, Gideon, and Seth stayed at the bishop's place for supper and the singing afterward. It would be exciting for the *Youngie*, to get to know the ones from the other district a little better. What must it be like to live somewhere like Lancaster County, where hundreds of young people got together for various doings, and the prospect of finding the one God had singled out for you was so much easier? Or difficult, she supposed, depending on how you looked at it.

Thank goodness those days were long over—those crazy, fraught days when she couldn't sleep at night, her mind working like a windmill as she tried to manage dating two boys at once. There were things about her youth that she'd been sad to leave behind—supple knees, for one, and the ability to run more than forty yards. But those particular nights ... *neh*, she didn't miss them at all.

Monday, May 2

The first day without Noah King at the Inn felt strange to Luke, even if he'd only had a few days to work with him. Noah was good company—cheerful, knowledgeable, and so much in love with his bride that it made the heart melt to hear him talk about her.

"We all thought she was engaged to my brother Andrew," he'd said. "But the more I got to know her, the more empty and desperate I got. I didn't know how I was going to be her brother-in-law when what I wanted was to be her husband."

"But it clearly came out right," Luke had said over his shoulder as he painted.

"*Ja*, with the help of the God of truth," Noah said. "Once the truth came out, the way forward just opened up."

As it tended to do. Luke couldn't help but muse on these Miller women. In each generation, it seemed, there was one who somehow got involved with two men. He thought of the boy he had been—with no immediate prospects, but enough love to work long hours if it meant being able to provide for Rachel someday. But despite his efforts, the scales had tipped toward Marlon Miller, and Rachel had chosen the man who had made her laugh, who was solid in the Lord and dependable as a rock, and who already had his eye on a property out of state where he could offer his bride a home.

Luke had been wild with disappointment and thwarted love and grief that she would choose Marlon over him. But deep down, he couldn't fault her for that choice. And so, when he had to endure the wedding at Marlon's side, he had pasted on a smile and done his best to support his friend. The torture of seeing Rachel beside Marlon in the buggy, or walking into church together as newlyweds, hadn't lasted long. After the young couple had made their move to New Mexico, his parents had decided to return to Wisconsin. Luke could have stayed. But his bruised heart couldn't take it. He'd boarded that train with a sense of relief that now the bruises would have a chance to heal.

He hadn't known then what a bruised heart really meant. That it would be like comparing a skinned knee with a broken bone.

He came back to himself an inch ahead of cutting a piece of newly painted trim the wrong length, and carefully made the adjustment. The thing about carpentry was that it required a man's full attention, even if he was only sanding something. The wrong cut, the wrong gauge of sandpaper, could spoil a job to the point it had to be done over. They didn't have time to do things over if they meant to meet Rachel's deadline eighteen days away.

Which meant he had to keep his mind out of the past and firmly in the present.

When he heard the bustle in the kitchen ahead of the bishop's visit, Luke dusted off his hands and surveyed the room he'd just completed. Creamy walls, nicely aligned trim and crown molding, the closet doors and the window trim and sills made of local Douglas fir varnished so that it brought out its warmth, the color of fireweed honey. With a cheerful rug and a bed with a warm quilt, this room would welcome its first guests with simple beauty.

There was a certain satisfaction in helping to create such a room.

He swept it clean of shavings, Sheetrock dust, and dropped finishing nails, and moved the sawhorses into the room he'd work on tomorrow. Then he washed up in the new upstairs bathroom that would serve all three twin rooms, and went down to let Rachel know he was finished for the day.

"But you'll stay for dinner," she said, sounding surprised. "My cousins don't expect you home every night, do they?"

"*Neh*, but with the bishop coming—"

"All the more reason to stay," she said firmly. "Granted, we both knew Little Joe during our *Rumspringe*. But that was a long time ago. It would be *gut* for us to get to know him as he is now, as a rancher and as our bishop."

He couldn't fault her logic. But something inside him warned against looking for opportunities to stay around when the bishop *wasn't* expected to dinner. Of making up reasons to seek her out during the day with a question or a request for an opinion. That way lay madness, to quote a play he'd once read —or if not madness, at least that rock-strewn path into the past.

Mentally, he turned his back on that path. "You might be right."

"Of course I'm right," she said with the same lift of her chin she'd used as a girl, getting one over on him again.

This sense of familiarity was dangerous, too. It reached out, sweet and tempting, and to stave it off, he said, "Can I do something? Put some wood in the stove?"

"I have no end of men around here, but somehow that didn't get done. *Denki*, Luke."

The stove in the kitchen had been tended to recently, but this house was built on the same old-fashioned but practical plan as several of the Amish places around here, with a larger stove in the basement that acted as an oil furnace might in an *Englisch* house. He descended the stairs with a lantern held high, observing at once that while the renovation upstairs had given the house new life and strength, down here it might still be the previous century.

Noah had taken the ventilation system into account, at least. The new piping and grates that carried the heat upward two floors had been installed before the walls had gone in. But the windows up near the low ceiling hadn't been deemed urgent. They'd probably been installed in the forties. And the stove might have been of that vintage, too.

"We'll need to get you replaced with a modern version, *mei freind*," he informed it as he swung open its front door and stirred up the bed of coals with the poker. "But as you're still here, you've got a reprieve—tonight might be your last night of usefulness, now that the weather is warming up."

"Who are you talking to?" came a child's voice from behind him.

He turned to see young Benny at the bottom of the stairs, also holding up a lantern. He was as sturdy as an apple tree, with Rachel's blue eyes.

"The stove," he said. "We have quite a lot in common. Makes for *gut* conversation."

Benny's forehead crinkled. "Stoves don't talk."

"You'd be surprised. For instance, you haven't told me you're puzzled at me, but I can see it in your face all the same. The stove is like that." He closed its door. "While we wait for those logs to catch, what does it tell you?"

The boy examined the old stove, its iron legs, the ball feet, the scrollwork around the door. "It's fancy."

"That's how the *Englisch* made things back then. Before I was born."

"Oh, so in the olden days."

He resisted the urge to laugh. He'd walked right into that one. "*Ja*. What else?"

The frown lines were smoothing out of the little boy's brow. "It has a name." He bent to look more closely. "G-glen-wood."

"*Gut*. You read well."

"Dat reads *Englisch* with us every night. Not just the

martyrs. Books about Amish boys and girls, and animals and things. Plus our schoolwork for Miss Christie."

"I like a *gut buch* myself," Luke admitted. "I used to like cowboy stories. Maybe that's how I came to cowboying."

"*Dat*'s a cowboy, too. We used to be ranchers, but now we're here."

"Do you like it here?"

Benny considered. "I like that we're all together. And I like Joel Miller. He's two years older than me, but we're cousins. He's from away, too."

"What's his *Dat*'s name?"

"Daniel. His *Daadi* is Reuben Miller, on the Circle M. I like it there," Benny added. "It smells like cookies and horses, not like paint." Then, as though this had reminded him of something, he said, "Know what? There's a chicken in the noble fir tree by the west door. I saw her."

"A chicken? Roosting?" She must have escaped a pen somewhere in the vicinity.

"*Ja*, all alone. Me and Gracie are going to catch her. Do you think she still lays eggs?"

"If you follow her, she might lead you to her cache."

The fire was roaring now, so Luke closed the door and lowered the flue. At the sound, the boy seemed to remember his errand. "Are we done with the stove? Mammi says the bishop is here."

Luke followed him to the stairs and had just set a boot on the bottom step when memory rose up like a wave of darkness and swamped him.

Seventeen years ago

"Dat! Me and Jessie want to come, too!"

Luke was backing the horse between the slats, doing his best to control his temper in front of the *Kinner*. He and Eva had been fighting since last night—despite the advice in the letter to the Ephesians: *Let not the sun go down upon your wrath*. It was like Eva had given up on their life together in the last year. Given up on him. She wanted to go home to Lancaster County, and he'd run out of arguments to convince her otherwise. But he was determined to try one last time on the way to the clinic for the baby's checkup, when they were alone. The baby, at least, wouldn't understand.

But Silas and Jessie would. With his luck, they'd probably want to run back to Mammi and Daadi, too.

"You can't come, *mei Sohn*," he said for the third time. "You have to go to Singers'."

"But I don't want to." His face reddened. "I want to come with you. You're probably going to the feed store."

Silas loved the feed store. Every visit was like Christmas to him, even if all they were going for was chicken feed, and even if his parents never let him browse among the horse and cattle medicines and poultry cures long enough. Luke suspected his boy was a farrier in the making.

"We're not going to the feed store. I've told you twice already. We're taking the *Boppli* for her checkup. *Kumm* now, help me with the buckles."

Sturdy little man, only nine, but so serious as he completed a task. If it had to do with animals, at least. Arithmetic and spelling words, not so much. That was eight-year-old Jessie's department—she was smart as a whip.

Eva came out of their shabby house, the baby in her arms. He hoped to fix their place up a bit when the money from the soybean crop came in, but for now, they were both relieved that their turn for church hadn't come up yet. Her face was stormy, but it brightened as Jessie skipped up to her, begging to come instead of going to the neighbors'.

"*Ja*, of course you can come," his wife said. "Go and get your coat. Get Silas his, too."

Luke swallowed down the hot words flooding his tongue. Trust her to know he was angry, to realize he wanted to talk in the privacy of the buggy. Trust her to invite the *Kinner* right in front of him, so that he would look like an ogre if he insisted they go to Singers' as planned.

He contented himself with a glare, which she ignored, blithe as any woman getting her own way. Fine. He would wait until the *Kinner* were in bed tonight, and simply keep his voice down.

The children bundled into the rear of the buggy. Eva sat on his left holding the baby, who was six months old and full of gurgling good temper. Luke shook the reins over the horse's back.

"The sun is going to be right in people's eyes, this time of day," she observed in the pleasant tone that was almost a warning. *Not in front of the children.* "Be careful on that left turn."

It didn't help that she was correct. But she didn't have to tell him the obvious. The road ran due east through a wooded belt where their lane came out, and at this time of year, the sun rose like a great orange bowling ball coming down an alley, blinding oncoming drivers until it got high enough to change the angle. Luckily it would be behind them on the way to town.

She and the *Kinner* chatted as they rattled down the lane, and he did his best to contribute a word here and there in as pleasant a tone as he could manage. There was no point in ruining the whole day for them just because he was feeling frustrated and shamed.

He slowed the horse and looked both ways along the empty highway. *Ach du lievah*, the glare! But no traffic that way. His eyes were still dazzled as he guided the horse into the left turn.

And the whole world screamed.

8

"Luke? *Bischt du okay?*"

Silas tugged on his shirt. No, Silas would never call him by his first name. Silas was—

But the awful orange light still shone in his eyes. Luke gasped and stumbled back, in the same moment realizing it was a lantern. Like the one he was holding.

Don't drop the lantern and set the house afire.

He blinked his vision into sense and saw little Benny Miller gazing up at him, eyes worried in the flickering light.

"Should I call Dat?"

He gripped the boy's shoulder. "I'm all right. I just thought I saw something."

The worry vanished and excitement replaced it. "Like a rat? Mammi will be so mad if there's rats down here. But maybe I can help her trap them."

"*Neh*, not a rat. *Ischt* okay, Benny. We'd better get upstairs and say hello to the bishop, *nix?*"

Luke dragged air into his lungs, trying to clear his head in the few seconds it took to climb the stairs. At least *der Herr* had had mercy on him and timed the memory for the stairwell, not the dinner table. His heart still pounded with the sheer cold terror of those screams. That sound had haunted him for years—in the north wind, in a hawk's cry, in a squeaky door. Every time he dared to believe that enough years had gone by to erase that raw sound, something would trigger it and there he would be, right back in the buggy with the left rein tightening around his hand in that turn.

He found himself shaking his hand as if to loosen the rein around it. Strange how such a tiny physical thing stuck with him when he'd lost big chunks of his memory for nearly a month, lying exposed in a white expanse of hospital rooms and guilt.

"Luke." Little Joe's booming voice shook him out of his reverie. Belatedly, he put the lantern on the table with its mates, and turned to his friend to shake hands. "*Gut* to see you. Didn't expect you here."

"Didn't expect to be here. Hope I don't interrupt any conversations you had planned. *Guder owed*, Sadie." He smiled at Joe's wife, who must have moved to the valley after he'd left. He hadn't heard her say a word on Sunday, but maybe she'd be more comfortable in a smaller group.

"There's nothing the bishop can say to us that anyone in the *Gmay* can't hear," Rachel said from the stove, where she was stirring something in a big pot. "Unless my *Kinner* have something they forgot to tell me."

Sadie laughed, and Susanna looked shocked. "Mamm! What will the bishop think?"

"The bishop's only thought is wondering what's in that pot that smells so *gut*," Joe said.

"Chicken and dumplings," Rachel told him. "And it's ready."

A feast was set out in the larger dining room where soon guests would be eating their breakfast, family style. After their silent grace, Luke passed mashed potatoes, roasted Brussels sprouts, creamed corn, and pickled beets. Rachel's dinner plates caused a riot of color on the table, the likes of which Luke couldn't remember seeing anywhere else. Even the little yellow bowl full of dried red chile fit right in.

"I understand the family will be going to church in the east district," Luke said, trying not to groan with appreciation of the fluffy dumpling like a cloud on his tongue. "Do Willard and Hezekiah meet on this side, too?"

His mouth full, Joe shook his head. When he could speak, he said, "*Neh*, they're on the west side. You'd think the creek would be the dividing line, but my predecessor made the decision and they don't object, so I left it alone."

"That means you'll be going to school over here next year," Tobias informed his *Kinner*.

Benny looked horrified. "Not going with Joel any more?"

"You'll see your cousin, never fear. But the school here is closer, and you can walk to Willard and Hezekiah's to visit the goats, then walk home," Tobias said.

With a glance at the bishop, Gracie said, "*Ja*, Dat. I saw some of the goats in our field yesterday. They seemed to be visiting *us*."

"Like the chicken," Benny said. "But I bet she's easier to catch."

Luke took a mouthful of beet pickle to cover up his smile. Gracie seemed to be the prudent one of this lively pair. No matter how she really felt, she'd never make a fuss about goats or chickens or anything else in front of Little Joe. He had the feeling both children held him in complete awe.

Which was a *gut* way to begin.

ADINA SENFT

"What about you, Luke?" Joe said, passing the chicken and dumplings to his wife. "I hear you're staying at the Zook place until the work here is done. But have you given any thought to what you'll do after that?"

"Don't be so quick to hurry him off, Bishop," Rachel said, handing Tobias the corn. "The work isn't going to magically complete itself the moment the rivers open."

"Gideon and Seth may have hired on at the Circle M," Tobias said, "but I'll still be here."

"I'm glad to hear it," his mother told him, "but what about the basement? Seems to me that's a two-man job, building more storage, putting in new windows. And that staircase?" She pretended to shudder.

"All right, Rachel, I get your point," Joe said, settling in to enjoy his meal. "Still, if it's ranch work you'll be looking for over the summer, Luke, the seasonal hands will be arriving any day. I can put a word in for you at Keims' and maybe that *Englisch* outfit, the Simms place east of them. Their spreads are big enough, goodness knows."

"Or the Rocking Diamond," Sadie said softly, as though she hesitated to intrude on their talk. "They're always looking for experienced hands to take the tourists up into the mountains."

"*Gut* point," Joe agreed. "Though I have to warn you, Brock and Taylor Madison are an acquired taste. I've known them ever since they bought that place and I haven't really acquired it yet. Reuben's done better than me. But then, they share a property line and Reuben is a smart man."

"Isn't Mr Madison the one you threw *Kaffee* at, Mammi?" Benny wanted to know.

"I did not *throw* it at him," Rachel said with dignity. "I was trying to help serve in the Dutch Café, and I turned too fast,

84

and there was his big old white shirt front just waiting for that *Kaffee*. Neither of us had a chance."

Her children grinned. "I still wish I'd been there to see it," Seth muttered.

She leveled a droll look at Luke. "If you do offer your services there, you'd best omit the fact that you know us."

Even Sadie laughed.

"I suppose what I'm getting at is whether you might make your home here with us," Joe went on. "I've got no call to hold you back, of course, whatever you might do. But it feels *gut* to have old friends about me. With you and Josiah and Paul, we have part of our old gang, anyway."

"We're not those boys anymore, Joe," came out of Luke's mouth before his brain knew what happened.

"For sure and certain, we are not. Our friendship isn't made of scrapes and escapades and cigarettes made of moss. But for four men whose experience of life has seen both storm and sunshine, I think we might have advice and strength to offer each other."

Luke wasn't sure how much of either he had to share from his storehouse of experience. None of his old friends had awakened in a hospital room to a fresh and living nightmare.

But he couldn't very well say that. He'd never spoken of it to anyone, and he certainly wasn't about to begin here, at the supper table with *Kinner* only a little younger than Jessie and Silas had been, gazing at him with that expression children got when they were trying to imagine their elders at their age.

"I expect you're right, Joe," he said at last, since everyone at the table except Susanna seemed to be waiting for a reply. "As long as I can find work, and as long as the goats can tolerate me, I suppose I might call the Siksika home for the time being."

"Glad to hear it." Little Joe beamed at him. "East district?"

"Seems odd for Willard and Zeke to be west, and me east, *nix*?"

"We need folks in the east," Joe said easily. "And if in the end you do decide to stay on for good, and maybe in time think about making a home with someone, you—"

The best dinner he'd eaten in a long time did a slow, sickening somersault in Luke's belly. Without conscious thought, he stood, pushing his chair back. "Joe—Rachel—sorry—"

He bolted from the dining room and out the front door.

❧

Open-mouthed, Rachel stared after him. "What just happened?"

"I don't know," Sadie said. "Is he all right?"

"I'd better go see." She pushed her own chair back, but the bishop raised a hand and stood.

"I'll go," Joe said. "If I caused offense, it's my place to make it right."

"I don't think he took offense, Bishop." Rachel glanced at the twins, whose eyes were wide as coat buttons at this unexpected end to their dinner, and changed the words she'd been about to say. "Please, I'll just go out and make sure."

"He's a grown man, Mamm," Susanna said. "He's not a boy Benny's age. I'm sure he doesn't need anyone hovering over him."

"There's hovering. And then there's being an old friend," she informed her daughter in a tone one shade short of her usual loving, companionable one. "Your father's *best* friend. Dat would have gone to see if he could help, so I will stand in his place."

Susanna bowed her head, her cheeks reddening at the reproof. "Sorry. Of course you should." Little Joe was already folding himself back into his chair. Susanna got up to clear the plates.

Rachel caught up her black knitted shawl from its peg in the mud room, and wrapped it around herself against the cool spring air. The sky was darkening in the long northern twilight, but the lemony remains of the afterglow still backlit the tops of the pines. A shape moved near the fence that separated the parking lot from the blackberry and rose brambles growing on the banks of the rushing creek.

"You should go in, Rachel," he said gruffly as she walked up, "and attend to your guests."

"The *Kinner* will attend to them. I wanted to make sure you were all right. Are you sick?"

"Not in body," he said. "I wouldn't want to waste that fine dinner."

After a moment, she dared to lean her elbows on the fence, keeping her posture relaxed. "But in spirit?"

"I'm fine."

Men. They always said that, especially when it was perfectly obvious they were not.

"I don't think we'll discover our friend Joe has taken up matchmaking in his old age," she said, gazing into the dark tangle of the brambles. "But I can't really blame him for wanting to see his friends settled."

To her relief, Luke leaned on the fence, too. Somewhere in the prickly, unpruned mess, a bird made a sleepy remark and fell silent.

"*Settled* isn't a word I'd apply to myself."

"But it used to be. Maybe you might get acquainted with it again."

"I don't see how. I've lost the hang of a job that requires me to stay in one place."

"Why is that?"

He was silent, and mentally, she berated herself for prying.

But after a moment, he said, "Early on, I thought that if I kept moving, my mind would be filled with new things. New people. New work that required brain power and commitment. But ... it turns out that memory finds you no matter where you are. Down in the basement before supper, it ambushed me. And then when Joe said that—" He cleared his throat. "I had to move."

More than anything, Rachel wanted to ask, *Memory of what? What happened, Luke?* But she didn't dare. Just a hint had made him flee outdoors. A direct question might make him collect his things and spend the night in the bus depot, ready for the first bus at dawn.

So instead, she said, "You didn't move far, I'm glad to see."

"I promised I'd stay and see the job through for you. I guess I forgot to add a codicil about dinner conversation."

She chuckled, appreciating the effort it took to lighten the mood. "I'll make a note of that in the contract." Should she say what she'd been thinking about on that topic, or leave it for a better time? Then again, what better time than this, when it was clear a slight change of subject would be welcome? "Want some other additions to that contract?"

"Depends."

"This barn raising. If it really happens June first, will you be here for it?"

"Makes sense that I would be. You'll need as many hands with hammers in them as possible."

"*Gut.* Did Benny tell you our fir tree is bearing feathered fruit?"

She could change a subject with as great a swerve as her grandson. "He did."

"Well, I want an aviary for chickens in in that barn. But the trouble is, the chicks are in at the feed store *now*. We need to get some sooner than June first, so we'll have eggs for the hunters in five or six months."

"Are you counting chickens before your barn is hatched?"

"I count one around here, at least. The point is, I need a temporary coop and run built right after the interiors of the Inn are done. And the fencing is all falling down." She gave the rail a little push with the heel of her hand, and it fell out from under Luke's elbows. "See?"

"I do," he said mildly. "Folks seem to be a little exercised, though, about my staying on here. Did you notice that?"

"Susanna and my cousins never learned the art of subtlety. You'd think they suspected I was engaging in behavior not sanctioned by the *Ordnung*."

"Which you would never do."

"Of course not."

"I'm sure your family will be relieved to know that."

"It irks me, though." It was still so easy to talk to him. Even if the subject matter skirted the edge of proper behavior, it didn't cross a line. "What if I *did* want to encourage thoughts of courting in someone? How is that any of their business?"

"It might be your children's business, to some extent," he allowed. "They'd have to live with the results of said courtship, whichever way it went."

"Maybe for a time. But eventually they'll find the person *Gott* intends for them, and make homes of their own, and then what? I'm prepared to live here alone, but what if I didn't have to?"

He blew a breath through his nose that might have been a chuckle in any other man. "You won't be alone, Rachel. You're not the solitary kind."

With a frown, she cocked her head in his direction, though it was now too dark to see his face. "And what do you mean by that?"

"Only that you're the kind of woman people enjoy being with. Your family parlor will be filled with friends and guests, and empty chairs at your table will be a rare sight."

She tried not to enjoy the compliment, but if the heat in her face was any indication, she was enjoying it all too much. "And the second thing?"

"Any man would be lucky to court you. Fact is, you're a pearl of great price, and many a man would be willing to give up his old life to make a new one with you."

But not you. You're not any man. Or many men. There was a time when I thought you might have been the only man. But you weren't.

"Go on with you," she said, turning and leaving the fence rail where it lay. "Come in and have some pie."

"I'll just replace this rail and be along in a bit."

But in the bustle and clatter of serving up dessert and doing the dishes and sitting down with Joe and Sadie after supper for a visit, he did not come back. And somehow, the warmth of home and company lost just a little of its glow.

❧ 9 ❧

Tuesday, May 3

"THE TROUBLE with chicks is that if you don't get them when they come in, others will, and you'll be out of luck." Rachel hovered around the riser containing flats of little fluffballs, consulting with Susanna and the twins after their return home from school. Her only decision was how many—a dozen. The twins decided on the mix—Golden Comets, Rhode Island Reds, and Susanna chose a couple of Buff Orpingtons just because they grew up so pretty and majestic. Rachel had no intention of butchering her birds after two years as some of the Amish women did—in her experience on the ranch, a bird well cared for was inclined to lay for several years.

And it had to be said that aside from their usefulness, chickens pecking contentedly around the place made an appealing picture for guests. She had to think like that now that she was an innkeeper, not a rancher.

The twins bounced on their toes, impatient to get the little birds home.

"We can keep them in the kitchen for now," Susanna told them. "They're only a few days old—they need to be warm, and luckily we don't have a cat to bother them." She let them peek into the covered box, causing a storm of peeping from inside.

"They are just so cute!" Gracie exclaimed.

"Babies are always cute, animal or human," Rachel said with a smile, collecting a couple of waterers and feeders and a five-pound bag of chick starter. "We can put them in one of those small packing crates with a blanket wrapped around it."

"We'll watch out for them," Gracie said eagerly. "When we're not at school, at least."

More likely they'd never leave them alone.

"I'm going to catch that hen today," Benny announced. "Gracie wants to call her Sunny. Because she's yellow and ginger."

"A good name. What do you think about putting Sunny in the box, too, to see if she'll take to them?" Rachel said as they walked into the Inn with their purchases.

"*Ja!*" Benny cried. "She's always hanging around the house anyway."

Gideon and Seth were still at work at the Circle M, Tobias and Luke carpentering upstairs. It was soothing to hear them in conversation between spatters of hammering. She and the twins got the chicks situated next to the stove and under a window where they could look up and see the sky. A couple of sticks of wood made do for perches, and goodness knew there was plenty of sawdust for bedding.

"We'll put Sunny in tonight, when she's sleepy," Susanna said. "I think she wants to be our hen."

"Remember that time we tried to put chicks under the Black Australorps?" Benny made a face.

Susanna pretended to shiver. "Don't remind me. They were so offended. We barely got the babies out from under them in time."

"Some creatures are meant to be mothers, and some just aren't, I suppose," Rachel said as the twins ran outside to locate the hen.

"Like Sylvia Keim," Susanna said, washing her hands. "I think she wants *Kinner* more than she wants a husband."

"You've figured this out, have you, in the two times you've spoken to her?"

"You just have to watch her, Mamm."

"No harm in looking out for the little ones. It's not likely they'll get into trouble at church, but there are creeks and gullies on every place, it seems, never mind the goats and cattle."

"Speaking of watching, was everything all right with Luke last night? He never came back in."

"I suppose. I didn't like to ask."

"Why not? You were out there for ages. And you all used to be friends, *nix*? You and Dat and him and the bishop?"

"We were, but there's been a lot of water under the bridge since then. He works for us. He does a *gut* job. No need for us to poke our noses into his business."

"I heard Aendi Naomi talking to Onkel Reuben at church." Susanna's tone was casual, conversational. "I got the impression maybe there was a little something going on between you and Luke when you were young. Before you and Dat got together, I mean. Was there?"

Rachel gazed down at the chicks, peeping happily as they recovered from being carried away, and exploring their new surroundings. "That's surprising," she said at last. "Naomi is not one to talk out of turn."

"It was only to Onkel Reuben. I just happened to be coming out of the bathroom and they were in the bedroom getting Deborah ready to go home."

Still. Rachel's peace seemed to drain away in annoyance that even her closest relations thought her affairs were worth talking over in public. In the quiet of one's own home, one's own room, that was different. But in the bishop's house, with everyone from church practically within earshot?

"So was there?" Susanna persisted.

"Was there what?"

"Something between you and Luke once."

When Rachel lifted her head, the smile fell from her daughter's face. "Unlike other members of this family, I do my best to mind my own business."

"Mamm, I didn't mean—"

"It's time to start supper. I'll go find the twins—they'll never want to settle to their spelling words after dessert if they're watching Sunny and the chicks."

She put a lid on her annoyance and marched outside, to find Benny and Gracie on the lawn attempting to herd an unwilling hen toward the house. "I have a job for you two," she called.

"We're trying to get Sunny to go in," Benny said. "But she's dodgy."

"It's not sunset. When it is, you can find her in her tree. Then bring her inside and see if she'll brood the chicks. But now, it's time to do homework."

Benny whined, and Gracie assiduously chivvied the bird, which only made it run around her and return to hunting in the grass.

"Now, *mei Liewe*."

They went inside—reluctantly, but they went. She would go, too, in a moment. Once her composure had settled.

She was not angry at Naomi. More surprised that she had known—or at least suspected—that there had indeed been something between her and Luke back then. The trouble was, she couldn't very well ask Naomi point blank without revealing that her suspicions at the time had been justified.

As for Susanna just happening to hear such a thing when she'd already made it plain that the farther away Luke was, the better ... well, best not encourage that conversation, either. She watched the hen yank a worm out of the grass. Susanna wasn't going to like Luke staying around to build a temporary coop, nor all the other tasks she'd set him. But unless her daughter was willing to pick up a hammer and do those tasks herself, she really had no grounds to complain.

But it did feel strange to have something that had to be kept from her only daughter. Something blocking the clear, running stream of their conversation around the house, about anything and everything that occurred to them.

Was this how it would be when Susanna became interested in one of the young men here? It was pretty common for the *Youngie* not to say a word about their courtships. Would she sense that her mother had kept something from her, and decide that she'd better do the same? The thought of not being in her daughter's confidence, hearing about a possible husband and offering advice, made Rachel feel a little sick.

Maybe she should tell her.

Communion was in a few days, the period when each one in the *Gmay* examined their hearts before they took the body and blood of Christ. She'd already heard Tobias's quiet voice in the twins' room, teaching them about the need for forgiveness, about making things right with your brother (or sister), so that one day when you joined church, you would know how to approach the symbols of Christ's sacrifice with a pure heart.

Is that what I am required to do, Lord? Tell my daughter that yes, there was something between Luke and me all those years ago? What good will that do?

She waited, almost seeing her own anxious thoughts swirling up into the wide Montana sky. But no answer came.

Instead, Luke stepped out onto the wraparound porch. Not quite the answer she'd been looking for. "Are you going to catch that bird?"

She shook her head and turned away from her fanciful, worried thoughts. "She roosts in that fir. She'll be easy enough to catch before long."

"Guess I'd better put some thought into your coop." He leaned a hip on the new balustrade. "I'd hate to have those chicks' ready-made mother eaten by a coyote. For that reason, lately I've taken to walking home a little early to make sure Willard's goats aren't out after dark."

Here was her opportunity. "Is that what you did last night? You didn't say good-bye."

He folded his arms. "I wasn't fit company last night."

"I'm sorry if what we said made you feel bad, Luke."

"You have nothing to apologize for. Nor does Joe. It's me. And there's nothing you can do about that."

"I can pray."

With a glance at her, he nodded. "I suspect you've been doing that all along."

She eased into the delicate opening with all the grace she could muster. "After I heard, I began again. I didn't know much about what happened. Nor do I want to know, even yet," she said hastily as his shoulders stiffened. "But *der Herr* knows. And we can trust Him to heal us in His *gut* time."

"Is that what He's done for you?"

The hen picked its way toward them, looking hopeful about what might be in someone's pockets.

"I believe so, *ja*," she said, realizing that it was true. "It look many years—as many as I expected to live with Marlon. I couldn't believe he wouldn't be with me to watch our *Kinner* marry and have families of their own. But *Gott* has plans that we know not of, and his death was one of them. I've come to accept it. With acceptance comes willingness for His plan. And with willingness comes healing."

She knelt down to the little bird, and to her complete surprise, it jumped into her lap. She hadn't forgotten how to hold a hen—her right hand slid under its feet, her left arm cradled it, its head poking out from under the safety of her arm.

"Look at that," Luke said with surprise. "You were right."

The hen's feet relaxed on her hand, a sure sign of trust.

"She wants company. A flock of her own—she'll make do with a human one, but today she's in luck." She felt a little bemused by the warm, feathery creature in her arms. Marlon's cousin Carrie Miller out in Whinburg Township treated her hens like this—not as food, but as companions. Rachel had always scoffed at it, being a practical ranch wife with growing children to feed. But maybe there was something in it.

"Will you stay for supper and see if she accepts the chicks?"

"Will that be all right?"

She had a feeling he wasn't asking permission. He was asking about acceptance. But from whom? It couldn't be herself. Her children? Susanna? "I think so. You're practically family, after all." Let Susanna accept that, the way she'd accepted the little hen.

Lost creatures deserved second chances.

He looked undecided, but since she was already heading for the front door, he paralleled her course around the porch and opened it for her. "Perhaps another time, Rachel. I was away yesterday and Sunday both. Will and Zeke might feel I've abandoned them."

"Well, you're always welcome. See you tomorrow."

How odd that she was the one who felt abandoned as his long stride took him across the parking area and out the gate. But she didn't get much chance to analyze the feeling. The twins got one look at Sunny in her arms and abandoned their spelling words in a flurry of loose pages and dropped pencils.

The light was fading in the window above the chicks, and their exciting day had worn them out. Gently, Rachel lowered Sunny into the crate, hoping devoutly she was doing the right thing. She didn't want the error they'd made with the Black Australorps repeated in front of the *Kinner*.

The chicks squeaked in alarm at the sudden intrusion, but some were so sleepy they didn't even wake. Sunny stood, stiff-legged with surprise. Then she bent to investigate the chick food. Ate some. Drank some water as though she was entitled to it. And then, having established her authority, she settled into the shavings over several of the chicks. The others wriggled under her and in moments, the peeps of alarm quieted into contentment.

Rachel breathed a sigh of relief.

"Good girl, Sunny," Grace said, reaching in to stroke her feathers. "You're their new mother."

"She won't peck them, will she?" Benny asked anxiously.

"*Neh*, not now. They've just become hers," Rachel told him. "She might peck *you* if you try to pick one up and cuddle it. But not very hard. She knows we mean them no harm."

As she'd predicted, it was difficult to keep the twins away

from the crate after supper, even though Sunny's eyes were closed and it was clear she was sleeping. Finally Rachel asked them to pull the blanket over the top to keep the light out of the chicks' eyes. That seemed to do the trick. Because as any child knew, pulling the blankets up meant you were supposed to go to sleep.

Tobias put them to bed, and Rachel tiptoed in to kiss them good night.

"I'm sorry Luke didn't get to see Sunny adopt the chicks," Gracie said sleepily. "It would have cheered him up."

How like her mother Grace was—so sensitive to others' feelings. So perceptive for a child so young. She kissed the little girl a second time and slipped out of the room. How Tobias must miss Lily Anne. So much loss—Marlon, Lily Anne, Luke's family. Had he really lost all of them? She couldn't imagine anything more dreadful. And think of the sadness he carried with him being perceptible even by Gracie —perhaps because of the depth of her own loss?

When Rachel came into the kitchen, she found they had unexpected company, and she was forced to shake off her sober thoughts and bring herself back to business.

Julie Stolzfus introduced the girl with her. Rachel smiled as though purple hair and a nose piercing were perfectly normal in an Amish kitchen, and shook the girl's hand.

"I'm happy to meet you, Alison," she said. "I hear you can help us with a—" Why couldn't she remember the word?

"Website," Julie supplied.

"Yes. One of those. Would you like some carrot cake? I was just about to dish up dessert."

"I'd love some," Alison said. "Can I show you my ideas while we enjoy it?"

"Already?" Rachel looked over her shoulder in surprise as she sliced the cake. "But we've only just met."

Susanna put the coffee on, looking intrigued. She and her brothers at least knew what a website was—the librarian in Chama had taught them how to use the computer there so they could place feed and equipment orders for the ranch.

"I know, but when Julie asked me the other day, I did some research. I hope that's okay."

"It's more than okay. Because I certainly have no idea what should go in it. On it. However you say it."

"On it," Alison said, laughing. She opened the silver sliver of metal she'd pulled from her bag and the screen came alive.

The men came in to get their cake, and stayed to gape at the pictures Alison was showing them. "But ... you've already got it done," Tobias said. "Or is this someone else's?"

"No, it's for the Inn," Alison told him. "It's called a mockup."

"My goodness," Rachel said weakly. It looked ever so worldly—and beautiful—and so alien she could hardly imagine such a thing connected with feeding fishermen their breakfast.

"So this is the home page," Alison went on. "These pictures are just placeholders. I can take real ones with my phone, but maybe you'd want a professional photographer?"

"Are those expensive?" Gideon asked, scraping up the last of his cake.

"A photo shoot could run between five hundred and a thousand dollars."

"For *pictures*?" Seth blurted. "I could buy a new saddle for that."

"Your phone is just fine," Rachel said hastily. "Would we be in these pictures? I'm sure Julie has told you that we don't like to be photographed."

"From the back or at a distance only," Alison said, nodding. "I think at least one is important, because it's a selling point. Maybe of you baking or cooking, Ms. Miller?"

"Call me Rachel, please. And I'm not sure I like our faith being a selling point."

Alison bit her lip. "Well, it is called the Wild Rose *Amish* Inn. But mostly it's the old-fashioned comforts of home, the family atmosphere that we want to bring out. Julie tells me you want to attract hunters and fishermen as well as tourists. Well, what do sportsfolk of all walks of life appreciate most? A comfortable bed and good, home-cooked food, right? That's what we'll show."

Rachel felt her ruffled feathers settle down.

"You'll want to connect to a booking system, I suppose."

Julie nudged her. "No way to review reservations."

"Oh. Right. So reservations by phone only?"

"*Ja.* We're going to get a cell phone from the phone place here in town," Tobias said. "I checked with the bishop. As long as it is used only for business and in emergencies, it can be in the house. Our cousins have the same arrangement with a fixed phone, for the cheeses they ship out—only in their case, it's in the dairy."

"The Zook brothers are your cousins?" Alison said, then glared playfully at Julie. "Why didn't you say so? I built their website, too, along with the one for the Rocking Diamond. My finest achievement." The girl's smug expression made her nose ring twinkle.

Rachel couldn't help but laugh at Julie's face and *Gott*'s sense of humor. "No one said a word. Oh, won't I give Willard and Hezekiah a hard time! I suppose they figured we would think they were as worldly as those Madisons, having a web …

site." She'd managed to remember it this time. "You just do what you think is best," she said to Alison.

But the latter was not finished. "What are you going to do about promoting the Inn?"

"Satisfied customers will tell their friends," Susanna said.

"But first you have to find satisfied customers. I don't think depending on drive-bys is going to do it," Alison said. "If people come this far into western Monana, they've already made reservations somewhere. If you like, I can do your social media, and maybe book placements on some of the Montana tourism sites."

She was speaking a strange language now. What were placements? "If you think that would be helpful," Rachel said. "How much is all this going to cost?"

Alison gave her an estimate that was probably a lot less than she'd charged the Rocking Diamond. At least, Rachel hoped so. But it was another world—better she pay Julie's friend for doing what none of them could, just the way she'd paid the shipping fees when the big trucks came for the calves in the autumn.

"This is exciting," Susanna said when Julie and Alison had gone. "Talk of bringing in guests makes it all feel real."

"Painting ten miles of crown molding doesn't feel real?" Tobias asked with a chuckle. "Maybe you ought to spend more time upstairs."

"You know what I mean." She nudged him with her shoulder. "She sounds pretty smart, that girl. How on earth did Julie meet her?"

"Alden Stolzfus told me Julie cheers for the local hockey team," Seth said. "She can't play, of course, but she goes to the home games at the rink by the *Englisch* school. Alison plays in goal. They won half their games this past season."

Seth loved hockey, and had no chance to play it or even watch it in New Mexico, since there was no rink within a hundred miles and it wouldn't have occurred to anyone in the Ventana high desert to build a homemade one.

"I guess you'll be another fan, then," Rachel told him affectionately. "Well, this has been quite the day. I'll do these dishes, and go to bed."

Later, as she settled to her knees on the braided rug beside her bed, she found she had a lot to thank *der Herr* for. Sunny adopting the chicks. Alison making a website for them. And Seth finding a friend in the *Gmay* who shared one of his interests.

I pray Your spirit of comfort will be with us all, Lord. Thank You for bringing me back to the Siksika, where I can find healing for my hurts and hope for the future. I pray for my Tobias, that he would feel it, too. No one can ever take Lily Anne's place, but maybe there is still happiness left in Your plan for his future. And Luke, Father ... I pray You would gently draw him to Yourself, that he can find comfort and love close to Your heart.

Just as the baby chicks had under the warmth of Sunny's feathers.

Just as a woman did the first time she kissed a man.

Rachel blinked her eyes open and climbed into bed, pulling the quilt up to her nose. Never mind going there, she chided herself. *Der Herr* had closed that door to her once already. She'd best not be trying its handle again.

Wednesday, May 4

"Mᴀᴍᴍ," Tobias hollered down the stairwell, "I think you'd better come and see this."

Rachel's stomach did a swoop and roll as she tossed the dish towel on the counter and she and Susanna hurried up the stairs.

"What disaster has happened now?" Susanna muttered.

"It can't be worse than when the washers for the faucets in the suites were the wrong size and sprayed water all over creation."

"Or the day Noah found that cracked pane in the new window just as he was about to install it."

That one had meant a delay of almost three weeks while a replacement window was shipped from the manufacturer.

"What is it?" Rachel found Tobias and Luke in the front suite, standing with their hands on their hips, surveying the room. "What's happened?"

Luke turned to her with a smile. "I think we're done. The

last task was to mount these brass numbers on the doors, and we just finished."

Rachel pressed a hand to her pounding heart, hardly able to believe it after all these weeks. Weeks in which they'd gone from snow to sunshine, from bare branches to leaves. And now, from shabby to shining.

She and Susanna took in the creamy walls, the glossy, warm wood of the window trim, the handles that would crank open the side lights. The plank floors, shining under their protective finish. The bathroom, small but efficient behind its pocket door, gleaming with new fixtures and an angled shower enclosure that made efficient use of space. Even the open pine shelving for soaps and towels had been hung beside the sink and vanity. And the numbers on each door shone with newness.

"You've done all the cleanup, too," she said. Not a speck of Sheetrock dust could be seen, nor was a finishing nail out of place. "It looks *wunderbaar*."

"Come and see the rest." Tobias put an arm around their shoulders and guided them into each room, including the shared bathroom that would serve the three twin rooms.

"It all looks so clean and yet so welcoming," Susanna said.

"The only decision we have to make now is when to go to the Circle M and get all the guest furniture delivered there so far," Tobias told them.

"And phone the mattress people *again* and ask when those will be delivered," Susanna said. "They promised the first of May, and it's the fourth."

Rachel had been watching the calendar pretty closely. You'd think that for an order of a king, a queen, and six twin mattresses, they'd be only too happy to be prompt in the delivery.

"You do that, *Dochsder*," she said. They'd got the cell phone now, which made nagging vendors much easier. They'd been walking over to Yoder's Variety Store to use the public phone in the rear up until then.

"I can ask if I can borrow the Zooks' buggy horses," Luke said. "We could make a couple of trips this afternoon in their spring wagon and your buggy."

"My kingdom for a barn for our own horses," Rachel groaned. "I'm sure our relatives are sick to death of us borrowing theirs every time they turn around."

"Soon enough, Mamm," Tobias said. "Noah and Reuben are getting it organized. You know they had to wait until the weather was reliable and everyone finished branding."

"People understand," Susanna added. "And our horses are getting their exercise at the Circle M, don't you worry. While you're doing that, I'll nag the mattress people and then unpack a few more boxes. I'm pretty sure we have more books than what's in the great room—all Dat's books on animal husbandry, for instance."

And so, before she knew it, Rachel and Tobias were trotting down the county highway in the big family buggy, with Luke bringing up the rear in her cousins' spring wagon. At the Circle M, Reuben and his sons were far away in the fields, checking the cattle before spring turnout, making sure the brands were healing well and there were no injuries that would hobble an animal and make it prey for coyotes and mountain lions. But there was no shortage of help in the barn, where Reuben and Naomi had had the deliveries stacked. Along with Rebecca, Malena, and Lovina, they were able to get half the headboards and bed rails on the spring wagon, with a couple of big braided rugs for cushioning.

"The dressers will have to wait for the hay wagon," Naomi

said, her gaze measuring their dimensions against the doors on the family buggy. "I don't think you'll get one in there, even through the back."

"I never thought to measure the buggy door, only the front door of the Inn," Rachel said. "But you know, they're so beautifully made I would have bought them anyway. Sol Eicher is a *wunderbaar* furniture maker—*denkes* for telling me about him." He and his sons lived in St. Ignatius, and had made all the guest-bedroom furniture.

The Wild Rose Amish Inn was Amish-made, right down to the bed rails. She'd better not say that to Alison, though, or she'd put it on the website, word for word.

"We bid on a dining-room hutch and a dresser for Joel at the school auction last August, and won them," Lovina said. "You'll see for yourself how popular the Eichers' work is if you go this year."

"I look forward to it. Now, what do you think about the boxes of new bedding? Those should all fit in the buggy."

They had time that afternoon for two trips. By the second one, the twins had walked from school to the Circle M so they could bring them home. It was just late enough that Rachel had expected dinner to be almost ready. But as she struggled through the door with a box of bedding, following Tobias and Luke at either end of a king-sized pine headboard, and the twins on either end of a box of towels, she couldn't smell anything cooking. And when she put the box down in the keeping room, she saw there were once again packing boxes opened in the middle of the floor, and Marlon's missing books on husbandry and animal care were half scattered on the floor, half shelved.

Well, she couldn't leave them there to be stepped on. Rachel shelved them, higgledy-piggledy, and went to look for

Susanna. The kitchen was empty, and given the fact that the sun was behind the pines already, it was clear her hungry sons would be having scrambled eggs and elk sausage for supper instead of the lasagna she'd planned on.

What on earth had happened to Susanna?

The bathroom door stood open with no one inside. Her daughter's bedroom door was closed, but when no one answered her knock, Rachel opened it.

The room was empty, the bed neatly made.

For the second time that day, her stomach rolled over with dread.

Calm down. She's simply run over to the variety store and lost track of time. Or gone to the post office.

But it was after hours.

In the kitchen, she peeked into the chicks' box. Sunny blinked up at her, already half asleep, her wings curved protectively around her brood. Which meant Susanna had been gone for some time. She walked back into the keeping room, half ready to call for Tobias, when through the window, she caught a glimpse of movement among the pines.

Something unwound in her chest and she rubbed it in relief. What was Susanna doing in the woods? The chicks hadn't got out. Was there another homeless hen?

Rachel hurried outside and across the lawn. When she was within earshot of the figure in lavender walking aimlessly among the trees, she called, "*Dochsder?* What are you doing out here? I thought you'd have dinner in the oven yet."

Susanna looked up as though she'd been awakened from a deep sleep. "When did you get home?"

"Half an hour ago. Didn't you hear us? Have you lost something?"

Susanna blinked. "*Ja.* It seems so."

It was cool in the woods, and almost twilight. Here, while the trees might have leafed out in their new spring finery, the grass hadn't quite caught up, and the ground was soft and spongy with damp and last year's pine needles. Their scent rose underfoot as Rachel joined her daughter.

"What do you mean? Come into the house. It's getting cool out here." Belatedly, she saw a folded piece of paper in Susanna's hand. No, an envelope. "Did you get a letter?"

"*Neh.* Nobody got it. I wonder if it would have made a difference if he had."

Rachel's eyebrows rose. "You're not making sense. Who is that from?"

Susanna met her gaze, and there was something in her daughter's eyes that Rachel had never seen before. "It's from Dat. I found it in one of his books."

Was she going to have to pull this out of her, word by word? "And who is it addressed to?"

"Luke Hertzler."

It was a moment before Rachel could speak, her mind was spinning so fast. "That doesn't make sense."

"Dat never sent it. It's not sealed or stamped."

Rachel took a breath, willing herself to stay calm. Any sign of impatience would just make Susanna close up like a clam. "Luke is still here—I think they're still unloading the buggies. You can give it to him."

Susanna seemed to snap out of her daze and defiance flared in her eyes. "I'll never give it to him. Dat never sent it—he obviously had second thoughts about that, considering the date on it—thirty years ago. And I don't blame him."

Suddenly Rachel realized what must have happened. "You read your father's letter to his friend? How could you, Susanna? I thought I raised you bet—"

"How could I?" Susanna's voice rose. "How could *you*, Mamm? How *could* you?"

And she slapped the letter on Rachel's chest. Stunned, she barely managed to grab it before it fell on the damp ground as her daughter whirled and ran out of the woods, heading for the house.

Rachel's first instinct was to run after her. Susanna might not be the twins' age, needing comfort or motherly wisdom to heal some small hurt, and she was old enough to manage her emotions, but it was obvious she needed to talk something out. Because she'd read someone else's letter uninvited.

She turned over the envelope, and there was Marlon's spiky handwriting, as familiar as her own. Addressed to Luke at his parents' old address in the Siksika.

She peered into the envelope at the top of the letter, just enough to see the date written there.

Five days before their wedding.

Honestly, Rachel. Close it up and give it to the person it was meant for.

But something in this letter had upset Susanna so badly she'd shouted at her own mother. Shouldn't Rachel know what that was, so that she could talk with her about it? And why, for pity's sake, was Marlon writing to a man he had seen practically every day, and who had stood up for him at their wedding?

Do not be tempted. Do not—

Rachel took the two sheets of paper out of the envelope and her own name jumped out at her.

She was going to regret this.

Dear Luke,

I can't sleep, so I'm getting my thoughts out of my head and down on paper hoping that it helps. I'd chalk it up to wedding jitters, but it's a lot more than that. See, I was told something earlier today by someone who thought they were being helpful. Someone who has seen you and Rachel at odd hours in the woods. Not lately, but before. And not often, but often enough. Maybe half a dozen times over the last year. After midnight, and just before sunup.

Now, maybe you were out there with my intended for some legitimate reason. Catching an escaped chicken. Hunting varmints. Or maybe not. I could ask Rachel, but I'm writing to you, man to man. Because while we know that gossip is the work of the devil, at the same time, it's put several things that I never understood before into a different light. Most of them involving the way she and you behaved toward each other. It never was the easy way of good friends. There was always an itch to the two of you, an unease, like you were putting on not liking each other to disguise the fact that you did.

Maybe you even love her. I know that you were disappointed that she chose me and not you. But Luke, once she made her decision, that should have been that. Seems it wasn't, if this person is to be believed. I don't want to think that the woman I'm going to see in church later this morning and then marry on Thursday has been carrying on with you even after she agreed to marry me. I won't believe that of her. But I believe something has been going on between you for a long time before that.

I want you to stand up with me with a clear conscience in front of the bishop and the congregation. I want you to stand up with me in front of Rachel. If you can't do that, then tell me and I'll ask my brother David to be my side-sitter instead.

Maybe I'll hand this to you before church. Maybe I'll tear it into a hundred pieces and throw it in the stove. I don't know yet. But what

I do know is I love Rachel with everything I am. I can only trust her, otherwise, what hope do I have of making a marriage work?

Marlon

HOT, STINGING TEARS TRICKLED DOWN RACHEL'S CHEEKS. Her breath was gone, the words like a blow to the gut, a shock to the soul. Like a flaming sword to the conscience ... *I can only trust her.* Marlon had loved her wholeheartedly. He was a man who could not help but trust the one he loved. And how had she repaid him? By keeping that secret room under lock and key in her heart. By loving him every day—but on this day this was written, it had been a love with a piece missing.

Twenty-four years of marriage before he died. *And he had known the whole time.*

He'd never shown her by word or deed that he suspected there had been someone else. And worse, that the someone else was the man he trusted as much as he did his own brothers.

Leaning on a pine tree's trunk, Rachel buried her face in her apron and wept.

She didn't know how long she was out there. Long enough for her throat to hurt and for the tissue in her sleeve to be soaked into uselessness. Long enough for the lamps to be lit in the house, their light enough to guide her out of the trees to the edge of the lawn.

A dark shape pushed off a tree trunk a short distance behind her. "Rachel?"

Her heart jerked in her chest. "Not now, Luke."

"Something's upset you. I could hear you crying. I didn't want to leave you out here alone, but I didn't want to intrude on you, either. Can I help?"

"*Neh.*"

"Can you ... tell me?"

She made up her mind. Pushed the envelope with its damning letter into his hand. "Here. Delivered thirty years too late."

He slid it into the tool bag slung over his shoulder without looking at it. "Does this have something to do with how Susanna is acting in there?"

"Probably."

"She practically screamed at me."

Rachel sighed. "It's best if you go."

"I was. And then I heard crying and realized it was you. So it's not between you two—it has something to do with this letter?"

"*Ja.* I'm going in now." She was so emotionally exhausted it was all she could do to put one foot in front of the other. "*Guder nacht*, Luke."

She was thankful he didn't reply, only saw her to the steps and then turned and walked off into the dark, his boots crunching in the gravel of the parking lot. She climbed the steps as if they were the final summit of some snow-capped mountain. One hand on the door handle, she swiped the streaks of tears off her cheeks with the heel of her other hand, summoned her last reserve of strength, and went in.

"What's the matter with Aendi Susanna, Mammi?" Benny, seated at the family table with his spelling words, laid down his pencil as she closed the door. Gracie took the opportunity to do the same. "She made herself a plate and took it to her room. Why can't we do that?"

"Because you don't have a table in your room." Rachel dropped a kiss on his hair and crossed the kitchen to where Tobias was frying up the eggs and sausage. "I'll take over, *mei Sohn.* You go help them finish."

"What's going on?" he asked in a low voice. "Something is wrong—she was downright nasty to poor Luke, and he didn't do a thing to deserve it."

"I'll talk to her," she murmured. "After the *Kinner* are in bed, or maybe in the morning."

She had no idea what she was going to say. She could only hope that the *gut Gott* would give her the words to help her daughter understand ... and forgive. Whether Rachel would be able to forgive herself was a whole other question.

Because this had to be dealt with. Much as Rachel wished she could just drop the whole matter in the creek and wash it away, the fact was that Communion Sunday was only ten days off. The contents of that letter could not be allowed to fester and grow and infect her relationship with her daughter—with all of her children. They could not walk into church and take the bread and wine with this between them. It must be resolved and their hearts and minds cleansed of it before then.

Rachel ate her supper without tasting much. The only thing she was aware of were the glances exchanged among her sons. Gideon even managed to ask if everything was all right, but all she could say was that she hoped it would be.

Because on second thought, shouldn't she talk this over first with Luke before she spilled the whole story to her family? He'd had so much to bear already in his life. And she should probably ask forgiveness for reading his letter. It was not, after all, like most of Marlon's mail she'd opened and read in the past—invoices and correspondence from the people they did business with.

On third thought—why should she reveal her innermost thoughts and feelings to him when he hadn't confided a single word of his own to her? For goodness sake, she'd been carrying the key to that secret room in her heart like a millstone around her neck all this time, when for all she knew, he could have gotten over her in a matter of months and not spared her a thought for the next twenty years.

She and Seth did the dishes in a pensive silence, and she went to bed afterward. What she needed was time with the Lord ... and then a dreamless sleep.

She managed the first, but it was a long time before she achieved the second.

❧ 11 ❧

W̲HEN̲ ̲HE'D̲ ̲FINISHED̲ ̲READING̲, Luke dropped Marlon's letter on the nightstand, feeling as though his friend had given him a hard shove in the chest—hard enough to make his heart stutter and the blood drain out of his head. Hard enough to bowl him over and make him thankful the bed was there to catch him.

Marlon had known.

He had sat between Luke and Reuben, had stood before the bishop with Rachel, had said the vows that would bind him to her for the rest of his life ... and he had known the whole time that she and Luke had betrayed him.

For they'd met one last time after she'd accepted Marlon's proposal. She had meant it for good-bye, but it had turned into one last kiss that had been the be-all and end-all of kisses.

Why had Marlon never given him this letter?

Instead, Susanna had marched in from her walk in the woods and shaken the book on veterinary care of large animals in his face—he'd actually thought she would whack him with it —and said through her teeth that it had been keeping his secrets for thirty years. He'd been completely mystified, until now. Maybe Marlon had used the letter for a bookmark and then been unable to get back to it. Or maybe just writing it all out had been enough and he'd closed the book on it instead of tossing it into the stove. Luke would never know. All he knew was that Susanna and Rachel had both read it, and the truth was out.

Marlon had known.

And loved Rachel anyway. Had married her anyway, had four children with her. Made a good, prosperous life with her.

She'd made the right choice, he had to admit.

And Luke had made the best choice he could in a field of narrow possibilities. At least Eva had never known that his heart was not entirely hers. He'd been the best husband he could be, the best father. And in time, he'd learned to love her. After Jessie was born, a new joy had grown in his heart that seemed to heal the old ache of rejection. He'd been able to see Eva as her own person, not merely a substitute for Rachel. They'd achieved happiness together in eight of their ten years together, before—

Before he'd turned left into the end of the world.

How was he going to go to work tomorrow and face them all? Maybe he should just cut bait and ask Rachel for his pay, then move on. Surely one of the ranches in this part of the state would give him work. If Will and Zeke would let him stay until he could get bed and board on a ranch, he'd have nothing more to ask of life.

He hadn't asked for more than that in a long time. He was used to it.

Thursday, May 5

AFTER A DIFFICULT NIGHT, LUKE'S RESOLUTION HELD FIRM. Following breakfast, his hosts got busy milking the goats as he set off across the fields to the Inn. He could have used the road, but he was coming to love the path that ran along the creek now that the ground was drying up. The trees had leafed out overhead, and he could swear he smelled some sweet flower, though he couldn't see it. The roses that overgrew the split rail fence at the Inn had leafed out, too, and their spiky buds were getting fat. They'd bloom next month, and the place would look a real picture.

The Siksika was at its best in the spring, for sure and certain. In the sunshine and greening pastures, a person tended to forget that Montana always held a trick up her sleeve. Blizzards had been known to hit in May and even June, as unexpected and brutal as Marlon's letter had been. No warning—and no mercy.

He arrived at the Inn, as was his habit, just as the breakfast dishes were finishing up. Susanna took one look at him and laid the dishtowel on the counter. "I'll get the rest of the books unpacked this morning, Mamm." Before Rachel could agree or not, she'd vanished.

He hung up his coat in the mud room, then walked into the kitchen, feeling as though he might be run out of there on a rail at any second.

"*Guder mariye,*" he said diffidently. "Rachel, I wonder if I might have a word?"

"*Guder mariye.* I was thinking the same."

His heart sank. So he *was* going to be run out. Well, whether he announced he was leaving, or she did, it all came to the same thing.

"I'll be finished here in a minute. Pour yourself a cup of coffee, if you like."

He did so with a smile that nobody saw, and ambled out to the wraparound porch. The section that ran past the kitchen door faced east and then hooked around the corner of the house to the south. Here, the sun had just glowed into view over the peaks at the far end of the valley. By the confusion in Seth's eyes, it was clear the Miller brothers had not been told a thing. Which was a bit strange—how else were they going to account for Susanna's behavior? Or even their mother's?

But that was no business of his. His business was to ask for his pay and be on his way.

In ten minutes or so, Rachel joined him, a kitchen chair in each hand. "Good idea. Seems warm enough to talk out here now, doesn't it? Make yourself comfortable. I'll see the twins off, get some coffee, and be right back."

He hadn't meant that they should talk privately, but if she didn't mind, he didn't, either. He listened to the bustle of the *Kinner* getting ready for school, and in a moment a buggy clattered into the parking lot to collect them. He walked around to look, and saw Rebecca King bend down to hug Tobias's children, then chivvy them into the buggy. School would be out in a couple of weeks, and then they wouldn't have to find ways to travel the five miles to school without horses. In September they'd go to the little schoolhouse a short walk from the Zook place, but he likely wouldn't be here to see it.

Rachel appeared a minute later with her coffee, just in time to wave at the buggy as it made the right turn onto the county highway. Instinctively, he sucked in a breath of alarm. But nothing happened as they made the turn. Hester, the Circle M buggy horse, clip-clopped past them, and small hands waved out the window.

ADINA SENFT

Luke relaxed his shoulders deliberately. Nothing was going to happen to Noah's wife and Tobias's children. It was just a simple turn. They were fine.

He took a sip of coffee. "I wanted to ask, Rachel, if we might settle up. I feel it's time I moved on."

"Oh, you do? For sure and certain, my daughter would agree with you." She sipped her coffee, too. "But I don't. You were never the kind to run away. Don't tell me you're going to start now."

"What do you know about the kind of man I am now?" came out of his mouth before his brain knew what it was doing.

"Only what I've seen," she said mildly, clearly refusing to be drawn into the kind of quarrel that ended friendships. "You keep your word. You work hard. And your work is *gut*. Beautiful, even. And at church, you didn't hide. I could see that it cost you to reacquaint yourself with old friends, but you did it."

"Well, when word of what was in that letter gets out, they might not be so welcoming."

"Why should it get out? And why would anyone care what happened thirty years ago? Only a few were even here then, and I'm sure they have scandals of their own to think over on nights when they can't sleep."

"Your girl cares."

"*Ja*. She and Tobias were closest to Marlon. She's taking it hard, and to be honest, I don't really blame her." The no-nonsense attitude faded away, and Rachel slid down a little in the ladder-back chair, holding her mug as though it kept her hands warm. "I'm going to have a talk with her. And the boys, too, probably. With Communion Sunday coming soon, I need

120

to clear the air between me and all my *Kinner*. Would you object?"

He didn't pretend to misunderstand. Nor did he hesitate. "To your talking to your family about the past? *Neh* ... though it doesn't reflect well on either of us."

"I know," she admitted. "I have to say, that letter was a shock. Susanna will have to ask forgiveness, you know, for reading your mail without permission." With a glance at him, she went on, "As will I. I hope you will forgive me, Luke. I've never seen her so upset. I needed to know what was in there that set her off."

"You're forgiven." If anyone had to read that letter, he would have preferred that it be only Rachel, the third side of their shameful triangle. Susanna's having done so added a whole dimension of guilty exposure to what he had forced into the darkness at the back of his mind. "But I think you have more to forgive. We might have been young and foolish, but I still had no right to put you in that position. Especially after you told me Marlon had proposed and you'd said yes. I was selfish and put my own broken heart ahead of what was honorable. And best for you."

"You're forgiven," she said, echoing his words. "You weren't the only one who was selfish. Wanting to have my cake and eat it, too. Only thinking of me, me, me. Honestly, I didn't deserve Marlon's love then. I had to earn it."

"Does that mean you deserved mine? The weakling who had no strength where you were concerned?"

"I didn't mean that, Luke." After a moment, she said, "What did you do with his letter?"

"It's in my room at Zooks'."

"Are you going to keep it?"

"I can't decide. In one way it punishes me. Us. In another, it humbles me to realize what a *gut* friend he was. I don't think I appreciated that enough at the time."

"Well, I think you should burn it. It's done enough harm, even though Marlon meant it for good."

She spoke the truth, and he knew it.

After a minute, he mused, "I wonder who the person was who told him? That they'd seen us at night, I mean."

She lowered her mug to one knee, gazing out over the split rail fence a few yards away as another buggy clattered past. Another witness to them sitting out here, all cozy and congenial in the fresh morning. Luke shifted uncomfortably and wished he hadn't fallen for its blandishment. This conversation would have been better inside.

"I don't know," she said in answer to his question. "I never noticed anyone hiding in the trees—but then, I wasn't noticing much in those days. Mostly I was just trying to keep the two of you apart."

"Wasn't like we only went one place," he said. "We walked all over, half the time not even aware of what road it was or whose fences we climbed." He shook his head. "Stupid kids."

"Speak for yourself," she said with a return of her old spirit. "All right, then, I'll go ahead and talk with my family. And you —I wish you'd stay on, Luke. I mean, of course I'll give you your pay now, if you want it. But that temporary chicken coop still needs to be built, and some work is left to do in the basement, and the fences need fixing, and I'll be putting in a garden soon, which means someone to break up the ground ..." She ran out of breath. "And the barn, of course."

When had he ever had the strength to refuse her anything? Not even on that last day—the day she'd told him she was going to marry Marlon, and he'd lost what little control he had. Some wild idea that his kiss could communicate what he felt, that she'd change her mind when she realized how much he cared...

Fortunately for them both, she was made of sterner stuff. She'd been the one to walk away, not him.

"All right," he said. "I'll stay and get the work done around here. Let me know when you've talked it over with your family. If I need to have an extra word with Susanna, I will."

She took a deep breath that might have been relief, and let it out again. "*Denki*, Luke. I appreciate that." After a moment, she said, "Were you happy? Out there in Wisconsin with ..." She stopped. "I'm embarrassed to say I can't remember if I ever knew her name. Or those of your *Kinner*."

Her innocent words rained down on him like hail, stinging. They might even leave tiny bruises. The fight-or-flight instinct kicked in, the way it always did when someone brought up the subject of his family. Neither Eva's name nor those of the children had ever crossed his lips once the police investigation had concluded. The coroner had deemed it an accident after his investigators had re-enacted the scene at the same time of day. The sun had blinded one party, and the other hadn't had time to slow, never mind stop. The fact that the other party was driving a big dually pickup loaded with firewood had no bearing on the verdict.

Only on the lives of those he loved.

The sun was up over the mountains now. Glaring at him. Blinding him.

He leaped out of the wooden chair and fled around the corner of the wraparound porch. And then down the steps to the parking lot. Where he found himself with both hands on the old split rail fence in the shade of the tangled wild rose-bushes, breathing hard, like a prisoner straining toward his only hope of freedom.

Except that for him, such a hope would never be fulfilled.

Rachel had learned over the years that nothing—animals, yard work, people—benefited from being put off, especially when the emotions were involved. So, after family prayers that evening, when she rose from her knees, she said quietly, "I'd like to speak with you all. Tobias, can you come back when the twins are in bed?"

"Are you having cake without us?" Gracie asked, shocked.

"We never get to stay up for anything fun," Benny complained.

"*Neh*, there is no more cake, and I wouldn't say that what I have to talk with your aunt and uncles about is fun," Rachel told them. "*Guder nacht.*"

She kissed them both, and Tobias took them down the hall to wash, brush their teeth, and to hear their own little prayers.

"What's going on, Mamm?" Gideon asked quietly, with a sidelong glance at Susanna.

His sister lifted her chin. "If it's what I think it is, I'd rather be excused."

"What I have to say affects you the most," Rachel told her.

"And if you don't hear it now, you'll hear it in your room later. I don't want to put this off until tomorrow."

"I heard you talking outside with Luke this morning," Susanna said stiffly. "Were you getting your stories straight?"

Seth made a noise like a startled horse. "That's harsh, *Schweschder*."

"Just asking a question."

"I was asking his permission to have this conversation with you," Rachel said evenly. It wasn't often she permitted rudeness, but if she reacted, Susanna would leave the room. Maybe even the house. "Since you read his letter without permission —for which I hope you'll apologize—I thought it was the least I could do."

"What letter?" Gideon looked from her to his sister. "What's going on?"

"We'll wait for Tobias."

The minutes ticked by as silently as though they were in church, until at length Tobias loped in and joined them. "Sorry to take so long. The little rascals thought they were missing out on something despite what you told them."

"We were just the same at that age," Gideon reminded him. "So. Mamm. What's this about a letter?"

"I found it yesterday in one of Dat's books," Susanna said. "Dat wrote it to Luke thirty years ago."

"That's what this is about?" Seth said incredulously. "All your huffing around and looking offended was because of some old letter?"

"I do not *huff around*."

"Five days before our wedding," Rachel said, plowing on before things got out of hand, "your father wrote to Luke, who was to be his *Neuwesitzer*, to say that someone had told him they'd seen us—Luke and me—out together late at night. I have no idea who this person was, or what they hoped to accomplish by telling your father such a thing, but apparently these sightings had occurred over a period of months."

"Was someone trying to cause trouble?" Tobias asked. "An old girlfriend?"

"We'll probably never know." She took a breath. "Because the truth is, I *was* seeing them both at the same time. It just never occurred to me anyone could be watching, with the crazy hours we kept. Luke knew about your father, but Marlon didn't know about him. At least, until this person spoke to him, or wrote, to tell him. It was the week before the wedding —maybe they thought he would change his mind."

Gideon snorted. "Not Dat. Even when we were kids I saw how he looked at you. And how you looked at him. The way I hope a woman will look at me some day."

Tears stung Rachel's eyes, but she blinked them back when her daughter spoke.

"Dat asked Luke in the letter if they'd ended it after he asked Mamm to marry him," Susanna said. "I'd like to know that, too."

"Seems like that was between Mamm and Dat, not you." Seth, her sensitive boy. Her deep thinker. He always got to the real point while everyone else was still flailing around in the weeds trying to find it.

"Well, Dat isn't here now, is he?" Susanna snapped. "But Luke is, mysteriously turning up just when Mamm needs him, and hanging around here day in and day out."

"She *hired* him to be here day in and day out," Tobias reminded her with some exasperation. "We wouldn't be finished without him."

"But she could have hired anyone. Why did it have to be the man she was two-timing our father with?"

Ouch. The truth stung worse than the injustice. "Susanna, it was thirty years ago."

"Still. You did. You were seen. And Dat knew."

Rachel gathered herself together. "*Ja*, he knew. And I didn't know he knew until yesterday, when I read that letter, too." She rolled her eyes meaningfully toward Susanna. "For which I asked forgiveness."

"What difference does any of this make?" Gideon wanted to know. "So Mamm was dating two guys at once. We think Amish girls don't do that, but I'm sure she wasn't the first. She could only marry one of them, *nix*? As far as I'm concerned, she picked the right one. She and Dat had a happy marriage. What I don't understand is why this is such a burr under your saddle, Susanna."

Susanna leaped to her feet. "Don't you get it? In that letter, Dat said he had no choice but to trust her if he was going to marry her. But it sounds to me like maybe our mother wasn't as trustworthy as he thought. Certainly not before the wedding. But what about after?"

"*Susanna!*" Rachel barely had the breath to say anything more, she was so hurt.

Tobias got up, too, and glared at his sister. "Who made you the judge over her? She's our mother, Susanna, and you don't get to run off your mouth, making trouble over something that doesn't exist. Of course she didn't see him after they said their vows. If you'd ever had a husband, you'd know better than to say something like that."

"*Tobias!*"

But his temper was up now, and it was as though he hadn't heard Rachel's shocked tone. "You're as bad as whoever was spying on two *Youngie* and tattling on them."

"I'm not tattling!"

She must get control of this before someone said something that couldn't be forgiven.

"Settle down, you two," Rachel said in the voice that had meant spankings when they were little, and time alone in their rooms when they were older. But they were adults now, her children. She had to speak to them like the grown men and woman that they were.

In a gentler tone, she went on, "Your father and I were here barely a year before the Four Winds Ranch came up for sale. Between our honeymoon visits and preparations to leave, we only saw Luke at church. Then we moved. A year after that, the Hertzlers moved back to Wisconsin, and Luke went with them to help with the farm. We heard he was married, and then ten years or so later, that there had been a terrible accident. But that is all I knew about him from the day Marlon and I got on the train to move to New Mexico until we all got home from Christmas last year, when I found that postcard from him."

Susanna rolled in her lips as though she was restraining herself from saying anything more.

"There," Gideon said to his sister. "Two kids grew up and married other people. End of mad, passionate romance. End of story. And hello, us. Growing up with the parents *Gott* gave us, and I for one am glad."

"Me, too," said Seth. "Can we have some peace around here now? And can we treat Luke with some compassion? He lost his whole family, from the sound of it. We should be caring for him like a brother, not being all suspicious and treating him like an interloper."

"He's taken time out of his own life to help us," Tobias said, his temper fading until he finally subsided onto the sofa. "I hope it's counted to him for righteousness. Because the truth is, this is a valley full of ranchers, not carpenters. Without him, we'd have lost Noah to that other job and it would have been Susanna up to her elbows in that bucket of wet plaster."

Seth grinned at the image, but Susanna only gave a half-hearted smile.

"*Dochsder*, Luke has offered to speak with you about it, if you want him to," Rachel said quietly. If this little talk was reaching its natural end, she wouldn't try to draw it out, but she did want to give her his message.

"I've got nothing to say." Susanna rose, but at least her tone wasn't argumentative or hostile. "Except that I'm tired. *Guder nacht*."

She left the room slowly, as though lost in thought. Gideon went down to the basement to put a piece of wood in the stove big enough to keep it burning through the night. Seth and Tobias went to their rooms, too, but Rachel wasn't quite ready. She curled up in the corner of the sofa where so often she'd nursed a baby or pieced a quilt or read a book when the house was quiet. Now it fit into their little family parlor like an old friend.

Gideon, she reflected, had been only partly right. *End of mad, passionate romance*. That part was true. The wild, self-involved, singularly focused infatuations of youth tended to burn out, the ashes blowing away in the winds of real life. *End of story*.

But was it?

For the first time in years, Rachel approached that locked room in her heart. Put her hand on the doorknob. Before, she'd only allowed herself a peek. Inhaled a memory. Saw him once again, felt him, heard his voice. Once she'd even done it when Marlon had been lying next to her, exhausted from roundup and sound asleep. Then she'd slammed the door closed and asked *der Herr* for forgiveness.

But after a while, she didn't allow herself to go there anymore, not even for comfort, not even after a disagreement or a disappointment, when it might have meant solace. Because she was wise enough to know that, as the years slid away, looking into the past was no help. And soon the past was filled with Marlon, and the ranch, and the *Kinner*, and things piled up in front of that door that made it just too much work to try to get in again.

Tonight, she turned the knob and opened the door fully.

The room was empty, and only shadows lay in the corners now. Even her memories had faded like old pressed flowers, losing their scent, their color and shape, and in the end, crumbling into dust.

Rachel shook her head at herself and turned away. And when she looked back, even the door had faded into shadow.

It wasn't likely she could find her way back again. And that was all right, too.

Friday, May 6

Hezekiah Zook set the plate of pancakes on the table with one hand, and put down a big jar of maple syrup with the other. It joined plates of fried eggs, bacon, and sausage. Luke's silent grace was filled with gratitude for these two men. They'd not only opened their home to him, asking nothing, but they fed him like a king.

Probably better.

"Everything all right, Luke?" Willard asked, helping himself to pancakes and passing them on. "You've been awful quiet this last day or two."

He didn't want to gossip about the Millers, but still, if his abstraction had been enough for his hosts to notice, it was kind of them to be concerned. "There's been a ... bit of agitation at the Inn," he said at last.

"Agitation?" Willard repeated, digging into his breakfast. "That a carpentry term?"

Luke huffed a laugh. "I wish it were that straightforward. No, I—" It was nobody's business but his and Rachel's. Maybe not even his. But like a stone tossed in a pond, ripples tended to travel outward whether you wanted them to or not. And to be honest, it would feel *gut* to talk things over with men he'd considered friends for a long time. "Well, maybe you ought to know. I'll be right back."

He fetched the letter and handed it over. Willard read it through, then, eyebrows raised, passed it to his brother. To Luke's astonishment, in the first few seconds Hezekiah's face turned pale, then as his eyes dropped lower on the page, scarlet. By the time he handed it back, he seemed so miserable that he couldn't look Luke in the eye.

"I figure my brother has something to say to you," Willard said quietly.

Luke's astonishment faded into certainty. "Was it you, Zeke?" he croaked. "Who told Marlon about Rachel and me?"

Zeke had to take a gulp of coffee. "It's been bothering me since you came back. And now with Communion Sunday coming up, I knew it was *der Herr* prompting me to say something. To ask your forgiveness. I would have, Luke, honest. Even without seeing this letter."

Luke didn't doubt it. "But how did you know, back then? And why didn't you just come to me and give me a talking-to?"

"Would you have listened?" Zeke's sigh seemed to come right from his boots. "I thought I was in love once. Of all the self-involved, blind, crazy times in a man's life ... anyway, if it had been me, I wouldn't have listened to some busybody trying to tell me I was being stupid."

He was probably right. Luke wouldn't have, either.

"I guess we weren't as discreet as we thought," he finally said. "Not if you saw us out there in the woods. More than once, it seems."

"I never would have if it hadn't been for the mushrooms."

Luke stared. "The what now?"

"Porcini mushrooms. And chanterelles," Zeke said, as if this should be obvious. "They grow up here in the woods in summer. I'd go hunting for them at night, after chores were done. Dat thought picking fungi was a waste of time, but Mamm loved them. And we loved what she made with them, didn't we?" He appealed to his brother.

"*Ja*, we did. After they died, and this place came to us, we made sure we kept Mamm's recipes," Will said. "We've always had more demand for our porcini pie at the school auction than we could ever supply."

"Pretty much cleaned out the woods," Zeke said sadly. "Anyhow, I saw you two kissing down by the river one time. And up by the big rock above the Circle M. Not every night I was out, but a handful. Enough to gather she had two strings to her bow."

"And then Marlon asked Rachel to marry him, and she nocked it down to one," Luke said. "We said good-bye that night. For good."

"*Ja*, well, I was full of myself then," Zeke confessed unhappily. "Self-righteous and all indignant that you could do that to a friend. Didn't even sign it, like a coward, just left it on his bed one night after singing at their place."

Luke picked up his fork and addressed himself to his

breakfast. Revelations were coming thick and fast, but if he didn't eat, he wouldn't be able to give Rachel a full day's work. "I'm glad you told me, Zeke. It solves a mystery, if nothing else."

"Can you forgive that young donkey that I was?"

Luke met his eyes and smiled. "I forgive the young donkey, and the old one, too, who's been carrying that burden all this time."

Hezekiah grinned back. "*Gut.* I feel ten pounds lighter."

"You don't look it," Willard said. "How many pancakes is that?"

"You know the pecan are my favorite," Zeke said. "It's your fault for making them."

They'd go on all morning if Luke didn't intervene. "When I get paid, I'd be grateful if you'd let me give you something for room and board. Those pecans don't grow on trees."

"Not around here," Willard agreed. He didn't embarrass Luke by refusing his offer. Instead, he named a sum that was reasonable in view of the amount of food they fed him.

When he left for work, Willard walked outside with him. "Rachel's a fine woman yet," he said, apropos of nothing.

"I won't argue with you there." Luke shrugged on his coat, though he'd take it off after the first half mile along the creek path.

"You aiming to court her?"

Luke lost his powers of speech. He stared at Will, his mind blank, his jaw probably swinging like a gate. Every cell in his body screeched at him to bolt like a rabbit at the very idea. Willard had no idea just how abhorrent was the thought of endangering a woman again. How even the kindest question about his family was like a fiery brand applied to his heart, his memory, his very being.

But he'd cut and run from Rachel like a coward yesterday. The least he could do for one of his oldest friends was rein himself in long enough to give him some semblance of an answer.

"She deserves better," he managed, and broke into a jog across the hay field. But whether he was running from Willard's question or toward Rachel, he couldn't have said.

❧ 13 ❧

LUKE SPENT the first hours of his work day in the Inn's basement, making a chop list and figuring out what he'd need to order. He was not hiding from the family, he told himself. Simply finding work to do before the shops opened. Midmorning found him at Yoder's Variety Store with the intent to buy hardware and fencing for Rachel's chicken coop.

"I'll have to order building materials from Libby, I suppose. We're low on scraps." He showed Abram his sketch of the coop. "Most of what's in the burn pile now is interior finishing, not studs and siding."

"I have a better idea," Abram said. "We can order in a shed, and you can put it together. Come on out back and I'll show you."

The display model was meant to be an equipment shed, with a sloped roof and square windows on either side of the door. "My girls got chicks, too. They ordered one of these, with six-inch walls instead of four, so it can be insulated. The boys tore down the old coop and built this on the spot. If I order it today, you'll have it by Wednesday. You'll need to lay down some gravel for a pad beforehand."

"I'm half tempted to advise Rachel to let me pour some concrete," Luke said. "That's a sturdy little shed. Nine birds would fit in there easily."

Rachel had no objection to concrete, though she was still set on a chickens' aviary in the barn, like they had over at the Circle M. Still, temporary or not, they had to figure out where to put it.

"I have to think about how it will look," she said, walking around the yard with him. "A clean coop doesn't smell, but a hen laying an egg might wake up a guest sooner than he wants to be."

"It's the sound of breakfast," he suggested.

"At least until a rooster finds us the way Sunny did," she said with a smile. "Then it's more like the sound of an alarm clock—at four a.m."

"Normal hunting or fishing hours," he added mildly. "Where does Noah plan to build the barn?"

She pointed to the wildflower field that lay between the Inn and the belt of trees that separated them from the variety store. "The Realtor told me there used to be a barn there before it fell down one winter. The bishop thought it might even be on the old plot plan—and sure enough, it was. Noah's showed me some sketches he's worked up. We'll need to regrade the approach from the parking lot over to the north end, where the buggies and horses would be. The bunkhouse and aviary would be on the south end, facing the county road, where both birds and ranch hands would get lots of light."

"And the room for church on the second level."

"With the hayloft."

He nodded, visualizing it, then tripped and nearly fell on

his face. A couple of ancient-looking stone steps led up to a small, flat area covered in mossy bricks and dead plants close to the kitchen door. "So until all that comes to be, maybe the coop ought to be at the far end of this brick part, close to the house but not so close that your guests will be disturbed by celebrating chickens in a few months."

"I think this used to be a patio or something, but it looks like the frost heaves got to it pretty bad." Many of the bricks pointed at the sky or were busted up altogether.

"It's level underneath," he pointed out. "In fact, instead of concrete, I can pull up the bricks and re-lay them. Clear out the dead stuff. Put the chicken shed I just ordered there." He pointed. "Then the run can go to the rear. It's got some dirt for them to bathe in, and grass to eat there, before it slopes to the creek."

She turned an appraising gaze on him. "I thought you said you were a cowboy, Luke Hertzler. When did you learn bricklaying?"

He shrugged. "Most men in our line of work can do a little bit of everything. You pick up something new with every outfit you work at."

"New vaccinations for the cattle, maybe. A new method of training a cutting horse. Not skills like you've got."

He didn't know whether to be embarrassed or pleased at this backhanded compliment. "I like to learn. I read a lot. Keeps my mind active."

She fell silent. As they gazed at the prospective building site, he heard the liquid notes of a red-winged blackbird in the wild rosebushes overlooking the creek. Another one—the female, likely—sang back. A pair of hummingbirds zoomed past their heads, no doubt heading for the wagon loaded with potted flowers that Abram kept at the door of the store, right where customers would have to pass it.

"Flowers," Rachel said suddenly, in the tone of alarm a person might use when they'd just remembered something vital. "We need to plant flowers around the deck. Soon. Today. They'll need to be established by the time our first guests arrive."

"I think your first guests might be more interested in the Browns in the creek than the flowers by the door," he ventured.

"But if their wives come—"

"Hallooo," a cheery voice called.

Luke turned to see a worldly girl, her hair an astonishing shade of purple and what looked like tiny jewels in her nose, approaching them through what might once have been a garden. "You look like you're plotting something."

"Flowers," Rachel said in *Englisch*, her eyes wide. "I only thought of marigolds around the vegetable garden to keep the slugs out. I didn't think about flowers for the verandah. You know, for that welcoming look when people arrive. When am I going to find time to dig up the grass in front?"

After belatedly introducing them and telling Luke that Alison managed the website, Rachel waved her arms and led them around to the front of the Inn. It looked perfectly fine to Luke.

"I don't think you should dig it up," Alison said. "Too much mud in spring and autumn. But I tell you what—a couple of nice big glazed pots would hold some of those wild roses out there. Dig a couple up and set them on either side of the steps. It'll look as welcoming as can be."

"Oh, you're so smart," Rachel said, clasping her hands. "Did you come to take pictures?"

"I did, but maybe I'm too early. Are the rooms ready?"

Susanna came out of the house in time to hear. "Hi, Alison. No, they're not. They're finished, and rugs are down, but until the mattresses come, we can't make up the beds. The mattress company says they're on their way, but I'll believe *that* when I see it."

No sooner were the words out of her mouth when they heard the sound of a large motor gearing down to take the S-curve that straightened into Mountain Home's Old West downtown. A big white truck rumbled around the corner, across their little bridge, and into the parking lot, where its driver reversed so that the rear door would open close to the house.

"I think I just became a believer," Susanna quipped as she recognized the logo on the side.

The quiet morning turned into chaos as Tobias, Luke, and the crew maneuvered the mattresses out of the truck and up the stairs, where they were distributed into the right rooms. Yards of plastic wrapping had to be taken off and stuffed into the garbage skip outside, which was going to have to be emptied sooner rather than later. Then Rachel and Susanna got busy with piles of newly laundered bedding—at which point Alison pitched in to help make beds.

"Oh my," the girl said as Rachel shook one of Malena's quilts over the king-sized bed in the suite at the far end. "Who made that? It's amazing."

Luke came to the door to see it—and then had to walk in to have a good look. Dozens of little triangular pieces flew around the larger design, and it was quilted in swirls of stitches that could have been meant to represent water or wind.

"My niece," Rachel said, her even tone telling Luke she was doing her best not to sound *hochmut*. "It's a variation on a quilt called Flying Home she designed for my nephew Daniel's wedding. God gave her a talent, and she was good enough to share a couple of her quilts with me. They'll be for sale, if someone finds they can't leave theirs behind."

Luke couldn't imagine letting something this beautiful go.

"Ooh, let me make a note." Alison typed rapidly into her phone. "This will make a fabulous picture. Can you scare up some cut flowers for the bookshelf under the window? And maybe a few books to stage it properly?"

Susanna headed downstairs to do as instructed.

Alison went on, "I'll want pricing for any quilts that are for sale. What a great idea, Rachel. Selling real Amish quilts at the Wild Rose Amish Inn. Who could resist?"

Luke figured the hunters and fishermen probably could— but then again, a nice gift to take home to make up for a man's spending a week away with his friends might be just the thing.

"It was Malena's idea," Rachel admitted. "I got talking to her when we went to get the furniture the other day. I just hope I don't take business away from Rose Stolzfus."

Tobias chuckled. "From what I've heard, I don't think you'll need to worry about that. Didn't your cousin Carrie say that Whinburg Township was arranging some kind of quilt tour, so that tourists could drive from house to house where the women had their quilts hung on lines in the yard? No one there seems to be worried about taking business away from each other."

"True," Rachel said, looking relieved. "Well, while we wait for Susanna to come back with the flowers, let's finish up the twin beds and Alison can get her pictures."

A comfortable bed and a little bit of furniture turned a simple room into a haven. Luke and Tobias had already hung the shades in the window frames, softening the look. Luke hoped *der Herr* wouldn't mind him sharing in the joy of creation, looking on what he had made and seeing that it was *gut*.

Susanna came back with a small purple hydrangea in a pot. "Yoders are loaning this to us just for the pictures," she said breathlessly, setting it on the bookshelf. She ran downstairs and was back in a moment with an armload of books. Then they all cleared the room so that Alison could take her pictures.

"This room will sell itself," the girl said with satisfaction as she moved her finger on the phone's screen and the room materialized under their eyes. "And the light just happens to be perfect on that quilt. I love this job!"

Luke had to smile. It seemed the joy of creation wasn't limited to the Amish.

Rachel invited her to stay for lunch, which inspired another idea in Alison's busy brain. "I know this is a bed and breakfast, but we can stage some of the dishes another time. What I'd love is to have a couple of shots of you and Susanna putting food on the table. Would that be all right?"

Rachel looked undecided, but Susanna clasped both hands over the *Duchly* covering her hair. "I need to put on a *Kapp*."

"I'm not—" Rachel began.

"*Kumm*, Mamm," Susanna urged her. "Both of us have to be in them."

Rachel's beautiful eyes turned to Luke in wordless appeal.

He had no right to advise her on anything beyond chicken coops and window trim. But he was no more able to resist those eyes than fly like a hummingbird. "Can't hurt," he said. "As long as the *Ordnung* allows photographs from the back."

He'd been in Council Meeting. The subject of photographs had been confined mostly to discouraging people from using their emergency-use-only cell phones to take pictures of each other or their children. But if it was for business purposes, surely Little Joe wouldn't make an issue of it?

Lunch was a rich New Mexican soup called *posole*, full of savory pork chunks and what looked like exploded popcorn, but which he was informed was hominy. Alison got a photograph of Rachel's work-worn hands cradling a bowl as though offering it to the guest, and a couple of views of Susanna from the back as she set out bowls containing biscuits, tortilla chips, and that red salsa that had already taught Luke a lesson he didn't want to repeat. The meal was complete with homemade bread spread thick with honey, and Mexican cheesecake for dessert.

"I'm going to be the first to write a testimonial," Alison groaned afterward, refusing a second helping. "You and Susanna are amazing cooks."

"I'm glad you liked it," Rachel said with a smile. "The salsa not too hot for you?"

"Not me. I spent my summers in Taos with my cousins. Honestly, I bet you could write a cookbook and sell copies on the website."

Now Rachel laughed outright. "That mind of yours never stops, does it? Thanks, but I'll draw the line there. We have enough work around here to keep us busy for a year without dreaming up cookbooks."

Alison departed after the dishes were done, already busy on her phone as she crossed the bridge and headed into the residential part of town, close to where the Yoder and Stolzfus families lived. Luke drifted out to the lumpy, broken brick patio, studying it to decide how best to rip it out. He couldn't put off the job, for sure and certain. The baby chicks—a couple of which had also been immortalized for the website

while exploring a convenient sunbeam on the kitchen floor—
had doubled in size already, and were flapping their tiny wings
and triangulating the measurements of the box for flight.

The scent of lemon shampoo drifted past him and he had a
second to prepare himself before Rachel joined him.

"That was quite a morning," she said. "Lots accomplished."

He made a sound of agreement. She had to know why he
was out here. But the simple pleasure of being with her kept
him from asking if there was a particular reason she was here
and not inside.

"I want to ask your forgiveness, Luke."

Surprised, he left off his determined study of the bricks.
"What for?"

"I said something yesterday morning that hurt you, and I'm
sorry. I won't bring up that subject again."

Color prickled into his cheeks. "I'm sorry, too. I over-
reacted."

"But if you ever did want to talk, you know I'm a pretty *gut*
listener."

He did know that, from experience. The silence flowed
between them, once more punctuated by birdsong, as though
they were getting a second chance to open up to one another.
Here was his opportunity to be honest. To tell her what had
happened that day that had ended the life he'd known and
catapulted him onto a road no man should have to walk. To
help her see that these jobs she'd assigned him would only put
off his inevitable departure.

Because once they were done, he'd have nothing more to
offer her or her family. He would move on, as he always did.

She had always been easy to talk to. Time was when they'd
talked for hours about everything and nothing. She'd never
betrayed his confidence, though goodness knew it must have

been tempting, since he and Marlon had been such good friends.

But what kind of man would he be if he burdened her with the past? What would be the point of filling her mind with images that even now made him sick and anxious if he looked at them for more than a second? In sharing his burden, he would only be adding to hers, and she had enough to contend with. The Inn, her family, adapting to life in a place that had changed so much in some ways it was almost new to both of them ... no, he couldn't do it.

"It's all right, Rachel," he said at last. Then he said some of the words she had asked for, at least. "You're forgiven."

She took a long breath. "I'll leave you to it, then."

He felt her absence in the air. The scent of lemon faded.

I'll leave you to it. His past. His work. His life.

It was best, he thought, even as his heart squeezed just a little in regret.

❧ 14 ❧

Saturday, May 7

THE NEXT AFTERNOON, Rachel was still trying not to feel hurt at the rebuff. Luke had a right not to share his business with her. But in view of what they'd been in the habit of sharing in the past, it was difficult to reconcile herself to a present where they were more like rancher and hired hand than old friends. More than friends.

That said, his forgiveness for her thoughtlessness was a relief.

She climbed the stairs to put the finishing touches on the guest rooms. She found Susanna in the king suite, collecting the little hydrangea for return to the variety store.

"Do they have other kinds of potted plants over there? And nice pots?"

Susanna nodded. "They've got miniature lupines, which made me think of the quilt Malena made. Are you thinking we ought to have living plants in each room? Not cut flowers?"

"It's a nice touch, *nix?*"

"What about this one?" She held up the hydrangea.

"It was perfect for the pictures, but those tend to outgrow their pots. We'd have to plant it outside eventually. And if we did that, winter would probably kill it."

Susanna nodded and took it downstairs. When Rachel next glanced out the window, it was to see her pulling the red cargo wagon along the road to the variety store, the hydrangea riding in it in solitary state.

Something inside Rachel relaxed a little. It had been the first non-confrontational conversation she'd had with her daughter since she'd found Marlon's letter. Her decision to talk about it had clearly been the right one. As much as the past belonged in the past, when it intruded into the present to upset people the way Susanna had been upset, feelings had to be brought out into the open, to be shaken out and smoothed again.

Not for the first time, Rachel was thankful that the prayer covering was a part of their tradition. Because the urge to pray could come upon a person at any time—as it did now.

Thank You, dear Lord, for showing me the way and for giving me the courage and strength to speak up. Thank You for my daughter and her love for her earthly father, and for the uncomplaining way she pitches in and helps, just the way she used to do in the barn with him. I only hope You have someone special in mind for her, Lord.

Rachel drifted through the guest rooms, folding the fluffy navy bath towels by size on the shelves built for them. In the shared bathroom, she filled a sweetgrass basket with unscented soaps and stocked the rustic cupboard with small bottles of shampoo and travel-sized tubes of toothpaste for those who might have forgotten them.

When Susanna brought in the flowers, she could declare the Inn ready for its first guests.

Now all she had to do was find some.

Back in the kitchen, she gazed at the calendar as though she didn't already have it memorized. *Saturday, May 7.* In less than two weeks, they'd open for business. She could admit only to herself that she was a little nervous about being an innkeeper. She knew how to deal with ranch hands, and with Amish guests in her home, but she had no idea how to manage *Englisch* guests actually sleeping in the same house. What if they wanted to watch television? Or talk on their phones late into the night, disturbing them all, but especially the twins?

No one wanted a pair of sleep-deprived twins in the house. Rachel had experienced that before, at roundup and spring turnout, and she'd rather not do it again.

She shook her head at herself. She'd made it clear to Alison that the website should speak as plainly as Rachel would herself. The fishermen were welcome to bring their rods and tackle into the house, but the hunters would need to lock up their firearms in their vehicles—or in a locker in the barn, once it was built. The Inn had modern conveniences like good insulation and propane and running water, but there was no electricity and no entertainment other than books, board games, and nature. If people wanted to be entertained with television and movies, they'd have to go into town to Talley's bar, or up the road to the Rocking Diamond, where they could empty their pockets of ten thousand a week for the privilege.

Less than two weeks. Well, the way Alison was working, she probably had the website operating and getting the word out already. She mustn't worry. *Gott* had directed her back to the valley of her childhood, and to this inn, and He would provide. She had to have faith in both *der Herr* and Alison.

Her gaze moved along the dates on the calendar. Next Sunday was Communion for the east district. The west district, which included the Circle M and the Zook brothers, was tomorrow, the schedule brought forward because of the joint Council Meeting. The east district had an off Sunday. Maybe that would be a *gut* time to have a quiet talk with Susanna, just to be sure there were no lingering questions in her daughter's mind.

The Sunday after Communion would be the first time they'd go to church when the Inn was open. With a sudden intake of breath, Rachel blinked, and stared at the calendar. Her stomach dropped.

Who was going to give the guests breakfast while she and her family were at church?

Oh, dear. In all the construction and renovation fuss, their focus had been too much on the building, and not on the lives going on inside it. Dear oh dear. Of all the times she'd stared at this calendar, how had she not made the connection? She'd been thinking only of the day when they'd have church in the new barn, not of the day next week when she might have paying guests in the Inn. Hungry ones.

Outside, a shovel thunked into the ground, scraping on brick. She hurried to the back door to see Luke at work, uprooting bricks and dead plants alike. He had been prying up bricks and stacking them to one side, already forming quite a little wall. The bricked area couldn't have been more than ten by twenty, but to her eyes, repairing it looked like an enormous project.

"Luke?"

The rhythm of the shovel stopped, and he looked up. "What can I do for you, Rachel?"

"I just realized something, and I wanted to ask your advice."

He looked around. "I'd offer you a seat, but all that was out here under the blackberries was a rusty old lounge chair, so I tossed it in the skip."

"It won't take long. The thing is—how am I going to feed my guests on church Sundays?"

With his forefinger, he pushed his Siksika straw hat up on his forehead. Like every cowboy she knew, the skin up there was pale in contrast with his tanned cheeks and throat. "You hadn't thought about it before now?"

"I've thought about church, and I've thought about guests, but I haven't thought about the two of them together." She tried to calm the flutter of anxiety in her stomach. "I was just looking at the calendar, and suddenly it hit me."

He chuckled. "Well, better now than two weeks from now, I suppose."

"It's not funny!"

His lips twitched, and she realized that this was the first time she'd seen a real smile. And there, appearing like a ghost out of the past, was that long dimple in his left cheek—the one she used to press a finger in to see how deep it was.

"I suppose you have the same options you had on your ranch when you hired *Englisch* hands." He leaned on the shovel.

She gathered her scattered thoughts and tried to look at his eyes, not his mouth. "And those would be...?"

"Well ... either they get up early for a hot breakfast with the family, or they sleep in and eat cold eggs."

"Would you be serious? I'd never let paying guests eat cold eggs. And I wouldn't want to use those metal tubs with little flames under them—too dangerous to leave unattended. Or with *Kinner* in the *Haus*."

"So, something that's cold? Or that they make themselves?"

"Rule number one. No guests in my kitchen." She'd decided

that long ago. She wished she'd had a better look at the calendar then, too.

"All right, cold it is." He gave her a curious glance from under the brim of his hat. "Did you never hire *Englisch* hands?"

"Sure, but if they didn't come in for breakfast with us, they fried up eggs themselves in the bunkhouse. Or had beans and bacon, or whatever else they bought. This is different. People will be paying us for breakfast."

He thought for a moment. "Cold cereal?"

"That's not going to sustain a fisherman for hours on the river."

"Cold meat, then. Beef and salami and ham. And hard-boiled eggs."

"Fresh baked bread." An idea struck her. "Mamm used to make a deviled ham spread. I could hunt up the recipe—I have all her cookbooks."

"Cheese—and homemade yogurt." He opened one hand. "Will and Zeke would be happy to supply you with as much as you want—and probably more."

She wished she had brought a pencil and paper to make a list. "*Gut. Ja.* This is making me feel better. As though I can solve this."

"Of course you can solve this. You're the most capable woman I know."

She tried not to let the compliment embarrass her. "You're kind to say so. But if I forgot something as important as feeding my guests on a church Sunday, I'm worried about what else I'm forgetting."

"Don't trouble trouble, Rachel, before it troubles you."

She had to laugh—it was one of his mother's favorite sayings.

"*Denki* for letting me talk it through with you. You have *gut* ideas."

"You'd have got there without me."

"Maybe, but it was faster with you." Smiling, she turned for the door, only to see Susanna marching back along the road at a much faster pace than when she'd left. So fast that the poor flowers in the wagon were rocking and jiggling like greenhorns on a trotting horse. "Oh mercy," she sighed. "Looks like Susanna's upset about something. I'd better go in."

Prudently, he didn't respond.

She met her daughter at the bottom of the porch steps to help her bring the plants in. "Oh, aren't these pretty." She'd always loved the lupines, and these miniature versions were every shade from deep blue to purplish-pink. "They'll look lovely with the navy towels, don't you think?"

"You owe Abram Yoder forty dollars," Susanna snapped.

"All right," she said mildly. "Eight dollars apiece seems reasonable."

"I'm glad you think *something* is reasonable. Because I don't."

"Susanna, good grief—what is wrong?"

"People are talking, Mamm. I heard it myself. I can't take any more of this. You are making a mistake and I just can't stand by and not say something."

So much for the return to congenial relationship.

"Who was talking? What did they say?"

"I don't know who it was. They were on the other side of the display with the pots." She picked up a little stoneware container of lupines and glared at it. "But it was three Amish women your age who should know better than to gossip."

"Gossip about what?" she asked again.

"About us! Our family. And about Luke working here, *prac-*

ticing to be the man of the house." With her free hand, she made quote marks in the air.

Somewhere on the other side of said house, the sound of the shovel faltered and then resumed again, more vigorously, as if attempting to drown out the sound of their voices.

"Maybe we should take these in," Rachel suggested.

Susanna snatched up another pot and a little of its soil flew out. Rachel clamped her molars together on the urge to tell her to be careful. Instead, she picked up the remaining three and followed her daughter's angry tread up the stairs.

"Honestly, Mamm, the renovations are finished. Luke is a cowboy. He should be hiring on with one of the outfits here, not playing in the dirt and hanging around." She went into Room One with its queen-sized bed and set a pot on the windowsill. "We need a doily or something so these don't scratch the wood."

Rachel did the same in Room Two, the first of the three twin rooms. "The potholders you made last year will do for now."

Marching into Room Three, Susanna said, "I know he's your friend—"

"And Dat's."

"—and Dat's, but people think he's not working so much as courting you."

Rachel took refuge in Room Four and set the pot on the bookshelf under the window. Maybe this wasn't a good time to point out that sometimes a man's hard work was just as beguiling as his courtship. No, that would definitely be a mistake.

"If they'd come visit, they'd see they were wrong," she said instead. "And then I'd put them to work so they didn't have time to gossip."

"Mamm, stop making a joke of this."

She stood in the doorway of Room Five, the king-sized bedroom, as Susanna set the last pot on the night table. "We can't stop people speculating. Luke is new in town and they don't know us very well yet. It's natural that we'd be the subject of conversation."

"I don't like it. Mostly because I don't know if it's true or not." Susanna paused by the window with her arms crossed over her chest.

"I think you do."

"If I did, Mamm, I wouldn't be so upset. How do I know what you talk about when I'm not around? I don't trust him."

Rachel felt a little winded. "Those are strong words, *Liewi*."

"I have strong feelings. I don't trust that he hasn't been carrying a torch for you all this time. Betraying his wife in his heart. Just like Jesus warned the people listening to the sermon on the Mount."

Whosoever looketh on a woman to lust after her hath committed adultery with her already in his heart.

"I don't think Luke is lusting after this old grey mare, then or now."

"Maybe not now, but he did before your wedding, didn't he?"

"I suppose so. It was a crazy time. Long ago and best forgotten."

"But that's what I mean. What if he hasn't forgotten? What if you haven't, either?"

She must tread carefully here. But somehow she couldn't. Not when the pot was so busy pointing out the soot on the poor old kettle.

"The way you've forgotten Stephen Kurtz?"

Susanna's breath hitched in a gasp, as though she'd slapped her.

Rachel immediately wished she hadn't given in to that angry urge to retaliate. To smooth it over, she said gently, "When a heart loves, *Liewi*, sometimes it takes a little while to heal. We've both experienced it now. But your father was the best medicine *der Herr* could have provided. I was able to see his worth as a man and as an example of how *Gott* treats us when we bring our broken hearts to Him. I wish you could know how much I loved your father, Susanna. How full and happy my heart was with him during the years *Gott* gave us."

But Susanna didn't seem to be listening. "How could you, Mamm?" she whispered. "How could you even compare what you did to—to what happened with Stephen?" A tear overflowed and ran down her cheek, and Susanna pushed past her and ran down the stairs.

Too late, Rachel realized what she had not known before. That her sensitive, emotional child had been hiding a hurt as great as any her mother had ever experienced. And how were they ever to come to the place of forgiveness now, before they were expected to come before *der Herr* with clean hearts next Sunday?

15

Susanna was silent at dinner and wouldn't meet Rachel's gaze. But she joined her siblings for the Saturday night Bible reading in the family parlor, talking quietly with her brothers and Benny as they waited for Rachel. But as Rachel came into the kitchen, she found Gracie hovering over the chicks' box when she was supposed to be in the other room.

"Kumm, Liewi," Rachel said quietly, holding out her hand. "Let the chicks sleep now."

Sunny clucked sleepily in agreement.

Reluctantly, Gracie stood and let Rachel help her cover the box. "Who is the chicks' father, Mammi?"

"I don't know. They came from a grower, so probably a nice rooster there."

"How come Sunny lays breakfast eggs and not eggs with her own chicks?"

"Because she doesn't have a rooster to fertilize them." Rachel turned the subject. "That's why she was so happy to have these chicks. She's a *gut* mother, isn't she?"

"What's fertilize?"

So much for that. "It's Bible reading time now, Gracie. Dat will help you understand afterward."

But, grasshopper-like, Gracie's mind had already jumped sideways. "Dat doesn't have a father, like these chicks. And we don't have a mother."

Rachel glanced into the family parlor, where the family was waiting patiently. "Sometimes it's God's will to draw His children to Himself in death, even if we'd rather keep them much longer."

"Is Luke going to be our *daadi* now?"

Rachel's heart seemed to stop beating. "What makes you say that?"

The little girl frowned. "I don't know. Chrissy Eicher said he was at school yesterday. She struck out at recess and I got to second base when it was my turn."

"Well done, but be careful you don't fill up with pride about it. *Gott* can't dwell in a proud heart. Now, come along. Everyone is waiting for us."

Rachel had to ask the Lord's forgiveness for her distraction as they read their verses from Acts turn about. Even Gracie and Benny read a verse, with Tobias's help. They were in second grade now, but still, words like *multitude* and *Mesopotamia* had not yet appeared on their lists of spelling words.

Susanna vanished into her room afterward. With a sigh, Rachel mentally girded her loins. She and Marlon had faithfully followed Paul's advice to the Ephesians when he'd written, *Let not the sun go down upon your wrath.* It was good advice. Because who could sleep when there was trouble between yourself and someone you loved? The danger of leaving it until morning was that the wounds you had dealt each other could scab over. Become hard. And that made the blessing of forgiveness even more difficult to attain.

So with Communion again on her mind, Rachel knocked on the bedroom door. A murmur from inside sounded like *"Kumm,"* so she did.

She settled on the end of Susanna's bed. Her daughter was sitting up, pillows behind her back, using a book as a desk to write a letter.

"Is that to Betsy?" In the Ventana Valley, she and the bishop's daughter had been friends—becoming closer as one by one their other friends among the valley's families had departed.

"Neh. To Emily." When Rachel was silent, trying to figure which of several Emilys she meant, she went on, "On Prince Edward Island."

"Oh," Rachel said in surprise. "Give our greetings to her parents. I enjoyed our visit, even if Christmas was a crazy busy time. Is everyone well?"

"As far as I know." Susanna capped the pen. "But you probably didn't come in here to talk about my penpals."

"You're right. I came to ask forgiveness. For bringing up Stephen. That was thoughtless and unkind, and I shouldn't have said it."

Susanna looked down at her writing paper, biting her lips.

"I'm beginning to think I was too hasty in brushing off the gossip you told me about. Did you hear what Gracie said?"

"All of us heard it. The parlor door was open."

"I wonder if Fraa Eicher was one of the ones in the variety store this afternoon."

"What difference does it make?" Susanna asked bluntly. "The point is, the *Kinner* are parroting what their elders say."

"The Amish grapevine is *wunderbaar* ... except when it's

not," Rachel said on a sigh. "There's nothing we can do. If we're a nine-days' wonder, I suppose we just have to wait for the tenth day, when people find something else to talk about."

"Or we let our carpenter go about his business and find work elsewhere."

Here they were, right back at the beginning, and Susanna had not said she would forgive her.

"Who will finish the brickwork, and build the coop and run?"

"Tobias. Looks like he's not planning to hire out. Not until the Inn is running."

"And dig a garden? And refurbish the basement? And get the lane to the old barn site graded?"

"My brothers and I can dig the garden. And you can ask Noah to arrange the equipment for the lane. The basement can wait until winter."

She had it all figured out, which meant she'd been thinking about this for some time. Longer than Rachel, for sure and certain.

"You make it sound like we don't need Luke's help at all."

"Well, we don't," Susanna said, stubborn as any mule with its front hooves dug into the ground.

"And after a full day's work at the Circle M, Gideon and Seth are going to come home and dig up a couple hundred square feet of untouched sod? And rake it?"

"It only has to be done once."

"And Tobias can leave his *Kinner* for someone else to take care of, so he can finish digging up those bricks and re-laying them, while he's completing the finish work down here and installing the counters in the family bathroom?" They'd been using the ensuite guest bath on the ground floor, which of course had been completed first.

"We already take care of Gracie and Benny," Susanna mumbled, clearly having forgotten all the items left on Tobias's punch list.

"The simple truth is that we need Luke," Rachel said more gently. "And more than that, he needs us. He needs paying work in the summer, that hopefully will see him through until he can find winter work."

"So you're going to keep him on, then."

"I am." Since when had Susanna become so unkind? Had her distrust of Luke made her hard-hearted toward him? Did she really begrudge the poor man making a living here where he'd grown up?

Rachel could see the truth in all her daughter's arguments. Sure, her sons could work twice as hard to make up for Luke's labor. Sure, Luke could hire on at one of the ranches. It wasn't too late in the season yet. But why should everyone put themselves to all that difficulty when the most simple solution was just to keep him on at the Inn?

She wasn't about to admit to anyone—barely even to herself—that she liked it when he was here. A little spurt of gladness welled up in her heart every morning at sunrise when she heard his boots outside on the steps. An adult around the place to whom she wasn't related and with whom she could talk things over was an unexpected gift.

"I hope you're counting the cost, Mamm," Susanna said into the silence. "And I don't mean his wages."

"I hope the *Gmay* have better things to do than peek over the fence to see what I'm up to," Rachel said. "Not that they can do that—our fences will fall over if you look at them sideways."

"Another job for Luke?"

"Low on the list. Some people think those old split rail fences are picturesque."

"They look awful now that the outside of the Inn has been sided and painted."

Rachel could only agree. But she still felt the absence of the words she'd come in here to hear. She couldn't go to bed without them. So she reined the subject back into its original track.

"I don't want our relationship to be like those broke-down fences, *Liewi*. Some things need to be repaired the moment they break."

At last Susanna raised her lashes to look into Rachel's eyes. "Have you heard anything of him in your letters?"

It took a second or two for Rachel to realize she meant Stephen, not Luke. "*Neh*, not a word. Not even roundabout, from Whinburg Township, where folks might have news from Colorado through the bishop's family."

"You think he might have gone to Colorado?"

Her eyes were full of pitiful hope. Colorado was just as far away as New Mexico, but at least there were Amish communities there who could be depended on for work and news. Rachel lifted a shoulder, trying not to reach out and hug her in compassion. "It's ranch country, same as Montana and Alberta. And as likely as anywhere to need a *gut* foreman. I hear there's even a buffalo ranch up Amity way. I don't suppose those are the same as running cattle, though."

Susanna's shoulders had slumped. "I need a little time, Mamm."

To get over Stephen? Or to forgive her for using him as a weapon? Rachel's heart sank.

"Let not the sun go down upon your wrath," she whispered. "Dat and I lived by that. I hope you'll remember it, too."

She couldn't imagine how awful it would be to live in the same house with unforgiveness. The coldness of it. The hopelessness.

"I haven't forgotten what my father used to say," Susanna said, without meeting her eyes.

There didn't seem to be anything else she could do. Rachel had no choice but to slip out of the room and close the door behind her.

The pain of not being forgiven was as great as the pain she'd inflicted on Susanna this afternoon. Maybe that was on purpose.

Saturday, May 7

Dear Emily,

Thank you for yours, which I got last week. I always enjoy reading your letters—they sound just like you! It has been crazy around here, but the good part is that the renovations to the Inn are finally done. No more living with Sheetrock dust—no more stepping barefoot on dropped nails—no more noise from dawn till dark! To celebrate, we went and got the furniture from the barn at the Circle M, and the mattresses arrived (finally). I think the mattress company got tired of me nagging once we got a cell phone. It's in the office (translation: the desk in Mom's room) and the number is 406-555-0954.

Last Sunday was Council Meeting. Little Joe (I agree with you it seems strange to call the bishop that, but everyone does) made it a joint meeting. This threw off the two districts' schedule a little bit. In the western district, the Circle M will be having communion tomorrow, and ours in the eastern district will be next week. Then everybody will be back on the usual every-other-week schedule. The good thing about a joint meeting is that I was able to meet all the young folks at once. There are sure a lot of kids here compared to the Ventana Valley! I stayed for singing afterward and was able to visit a little with my cousins. Ruby Wengerd sends her best greetings. I hope your brother Cale has recovered from his crush on her. She and Zach are so funny, sitting next to each other not saying a word, as happy as can be. I suppose they do talk when they're alone. I hope so, anyway.

The week before Council Meeting, we took on a hired man called Luke Hertzler. I don't suppose you would have heard talk about him, but apparently something awful happened to his family years ago and he's been cowboying alone ever since. He grew up here, and I've recently found out that he used to date my mother. Worse, he dated her at the same time she was dating Dad! Imagine how you'd feel if you found out your mother had two-timed your father before she married him. I found a letter in one of Dad's books addressed to Luke, and that really set off a storm.

Because Dad knew about their behavior and never told anyone— not even Mom!

I'm so verhuddelt—yes, I have to use a Dutch word, there isn't an equivalent for how I feel in English—I can hardly think. I'm afraid there's been some harsh words around here, most of them coming out of my mouth. But I can't seem to get over it. And then Mom threw my ex in my face, like there was some kind of comparison between two-timing and being dumped. I'm just so mad at her I can hardly speak.

She just came into my room to ask me to forgive her, but I know perfectly well it's because Communion is next weekend, and she wants things to be all neat and tidy, not because she's sorry.

How do I know that, you ask? Because if she _was_ sorry, she'd send Luke on his way. How do we know there isn't still something there? I've seen the way he looks at her, and she's always out there talking to him. I feel like she not only betrayed my father during his lifetime, she's betraying him now that he's dead, too.

Honestly, I'm half tempted to get on a train and come out to PEI *for a good long visit. What route would you recommend? Either that, or I could move to the Circle M. Except they won't have a bedroom free until Noah and Rebecca build a place of their own. Or Adam and Zach get their houses built so they can get married and move out.*

Sorry to be such a whiner. It's nice to have someone to talk to who's far enough away that I can be sure word won't get back to my mother! You can bet I hide your letters, too, in a box on the top shelf of my closet. This inn is a century old—you'd think there'd be a handy board I could tilt up to hide things under. But not after the renovation. Noah and Tobias are nothing if not thorough. Believe me, I know from experience how hard it is to get over someone you thought really cared about you. Looks like both of us were dumped on our heads around the same time—though I have to say, it's got to be more painful when the person you cared for marries someone else so fast. When you said it was hardest to come to terms with the fact that you didn't really know him at all, it really hit home for me.

I thought I knew Stephen so well—he was our foreman on the Four Winds. You should have seen him—tall, dark, and handsome doesn't begin to describe it. But mostly it was his eyes. He seemed to see me the way I wish I was instead of the way I really am, if that makes sense. But maybe that was the problem. The real me apparently wasn't who he wanted, right? He just up and left one day, when Mom first started talking about moving. He waited until roundup was over—waited exactly one day. And then he and his duffel bag and saddle were gone, and he hasn't been heard from since. Not even a good-bye. Well, he said good-bye to Mom when he collected his final pay envelope and gave his two minutes' notice, but that was it. I never saw him leave. Maybe he meant it that way.

So here I am, doing my best not to think about him, and Mom throws him in my face.

All right, I'll stop crying on your shoulder now. I'll bear up like I always do, and smile, and go to singing like I could actually muster any interest in the young men here. (Calvin Yoder—ugh! I can't believe he flirted with you and then turned around and tried it on me! Does he think we don't talk?)

I'll be glad when the Inn opens. Having guests around and lots to do will hopefully help with my state of mind. And if it gets to be too much, maybe one of these days you'll get a phone call from the Charlottetown bus station and it will be me!

Love from your sister in Christ,
Susanna

16

Wednesday, May 11

THE DELIVERY TRUCK from Libby rumbled into the Inn's parking lot, where Luke and Tobias helped the driver unload the prefab chicken coop. From the tangled old garden, Rachel paused in her cutting and digging to watch them carry the pieces past her piles of dead plants to the newly completed patio, which Luke had reconstructed in a beautiful herringbone pattern, surrounded by a quadrangle of shallow walls so the bricks didn't travel in their bed of sand.

That part, at least, lived up to the beauty of the renovated Inn. She went back to work on the neglected flower garden.

"Nice," the driver said, dusting off his hands. "Are you sure this is where you want the shed, in this corner? Seems like patio furniture and a picnic table would be better."

"Until December, maybe," Tobias said mildly, "when we might be pretty thankful we only have to shovel a ten-foot path right outside the kitchen door."

The driver laughed, had him sign for the delivery, and

rumbled off to the variety store, which seemed to be doing a good business in small sheds, if the three remaining on the truck bed were any indication.

Luke and Tobias got to work, and by the end of the school day, not only had Rachel got the kitchen garden cleared out and some cooking herbs seeded or planted, but the new shed was built, too. It stood at the near end of its newly fenced and roofed enclosure, which could be accessed through its door. The enclosure encompassed several square feet of grass so that the chickens could graze, as well as a wooden box up against the low wall, filled with all the leftover sand so that they could have the dust baths they needed to keep themselves clean. The men had laid bricks on end around the enclosure, too, sunk into the soil, to keep predators from digging under it, and the metal roof would provide shelter from snow and rain as well as protection from hawks.

Rachel couldn't help a grin at the sheer excitement of Gracie and Benny when they jumped down from the buggy driven by Noah King, his wife at his side, who had given them a ride home. The young couple joined her to watch the ceremonious transport of the nursery box to the new coop. With Tobias keeping a close eye on the proceedings in there, Luke came over to gather up Rachel's piles for the compost heap over by the planned site of her vegetable garden, out of their future guests' view.

By the time he came back, dusting off his hands, she had given the Kings a quick tour of the furnished and decorated guest rooms. Then, as Luke put away the construction tools and located his coat, she realized that *Gott* had sent her an unexpected opportunity to speak to them together.

"Rebecca, Noah—I wonder if you have a few minutes to take a walk with me?"

Rebecca looked surprised, but Noah only said, "Sure. We have an hour before Naomi expects us back for supper."

"An hour will be just enough." She glanced at Luke. "All right if we walk partway home with you?"

She saw at once that he understood what she meant to do, since the route would take them right past the L-shaped parcel of land. "I'd be happy for the company," was all he said.

They crossed the creek by the Inn's bridge, but only stayed on the road for a quarter mile or so. Then Luke led them along the path that meandered along the creek's eastern bank. "I've worn this path a little deeper since I started work at the Inn," he explained over his shoulder. "I'm enjoying it because it's never the same. Every day something new has grown or hatched."

Rachel didn't walk it much, being too busy at home, but even she could see the differences now that summer was taking hold. The grass sprang out of the soil as though it knew it didn't have much time to grow and seed itself for next year. Dozens of buds on the wild rose bushes were going to explode into pink blossom any second. And, like a surprise bouquet, here and there were clusters of arrowleaf balsamroot with their brilliant gold daisylike flowers.

The path bent around a cluster of boulders, where a new white stake had been driven into the ground. Another was visible up by the road, and a third peeked above the grass on the far side of the field, where the Zook brothers' property line ran. The path Luke had worn through the field on his way to the Inn was also visible, but they stopped there, by the boulders.

"The county surveyor was here on Monday, surveying this parcel," Rachel said casually. "It's an odd bit of land, shaped like an L." She pointed toward the road, drawing it with one hand. "These boulders mark the angle of the L, and then it continues over there. I was talking with Willard and Hezekiah not long ago, and they agreed there wasn't much a person could do with it, other than plant it in hay, or maybe sell it for a house and shop."

"What do you plan to do?" Noah asked after a moment, as if hesitant to poke into her business. "Seems like hay would be sensible."

"I've got about fifteen acres in hay between here and the Inn. I reckon that's enough." Rachel took a breath. "But I don't want to sell it. You may have noticed, Noah, that I haven't paid you yet for all your work."

He laughed, and Rebecca looked uncomfortable. "I did notice, but I figured you'd get to it eventually, once you had the Inn ready for guests."

"Well, I've got to it now. I wonder if you'd accept this funny little piece of land in lieu of payment. And as a wedding gift."

Noah's jaw dropped, and Rebecca turned pale, then blushed scarlet. "Aendi Rachel—"

Rachel almost felt sorry for them. Maybe she ought to have led up to the subject a little more gently. "I know you're saving up to buy property. I didn't figure you'd be bidding on any thousand-acre ranches, but instead opening a carpentry shop close to your home. This piece has got an odd shape, but there's plenty of room for a shop up there by the road."

Luke added in his diffident way, "I wouldn't put a house here by the creek, where it's prone to flooding, but there's good drainage on that slope, and a house could go over there, where the stake is. It's up to you, of course."

"My cousins wanted me to warn you that the goats tend to

escape periodically, but that's the only flaw they could see with my plan," Rachel told them.

Noah finally recovered his powers of speech. "You've talked it over with them? Don't they want to buy it, if you're selling?"

"They figured they'd rather have you two as neighbors than own it themselves," Rachel said with a smile.

Rebecca's breath hitched, and tears overflowed her eyes. "Oh, Aendi Rachel, I don't know what to say."

"Ach, Liewi." Rachel gathered her niece into her arms, and the slender shoulders shook with sobs of gratitude. "I hope your *Mann* will say yes. Otherwise I might have to take out a bank loan to repay him for all he's done. He's gone above and beyond in making the Inn something special. If a laborer is worthy of his hire, then this little piece of land can't even do that. But it's what I've got, and the two of you are welcome to it."

"But Tobias—Rebecca's cousins—won't they want it when the time comes?" Noah sounded winded.

"They say they don't," Rachel told him. Rebecca was doing her best to calm the storm of her emotion, pulling back to take refuge in the circle of Noah's arms. She dug in the pockets of her apron for a tissue. Rachel handed her the one perpetually up her sleeve, and the girl blew her nose. When she lifted her head, her eyes were shining as she gazed over the meadows and the slope up to the road.

Noah chuckled. "It seems *mei Fraa* has fallen in love with something besides me." He kissed her temple.

"Then you'd better say yes," Rachel prompted.

And now it was Noah in Rachel's arms, the heat in his face against her shoulder betraying his own emotion. When he lifted his head from her hug, his eyes were wet. "I don't have words to thank you enough, Aendi. It's worth far more than the wages."

"I disagree. It will give you a start to both home and business. This is what I want, Noah. It's what your cousins want, too."

"Best say yes, my friend," Luke advised from where he watched the rush of the creek. "Your aunt is a mighty determined woman."

"I know she is." Noah scrubbed the moisture from his cheeks and took Rebecca's hand. "We don't deserve it, but we'll do our best to live up to your confidence in us. We'd be glad and honored to be your neighbors. And Will and Zeke's, too."

Rachel couldn't help her smile, big enough to make her face hurt, as she kissed them both. "That's settled, then. We'll pay a visit to the town office whenever it's convenient and I'll deed it over to you. Then you can add one more job to your list of construction projects."

"It'll be hard not to put it right at the top," Noah said wryly. "But we've been dreaming and planning for something like this since we were engaged. We thought it would be a fixer-upper in town somewhere. We never thought of buying land—couldn't afford it."

Rebecca gazed up into his face. "I'm going to talk to Zach tonight, and ask him to draw us just the kind of house we've dreamed of. That will make it seem all the more real, though those white stakes are as real as real gets."

"Once the county puts it on paper, it's real," Rachel agreed. Then she turned to Luke. "Tell my cousins they'd better start training their goats to better manners, starting today."

"I'll do that," he said, nodding. "They'll be pleased. *Guder owed*, all. I'll be heading for my own supper now."

As Rachel walked home with her niece and nephew-in-law, then saw them off, already chattering excitedly as the buggy rolled back across the bridge, she felt the difference in their situations. A young couple, leaving together in possession of a gift that would make a difference to their entire future. And here she was, alone with the Inn that was her own future. As she'd planned.

But ...

For just a moment, as Luke had turned away and walked through the ankle-high young hay toward the Zook fence line, she had felt the separation. As though her being alone and his being alone were no longer right.

Could it even be made right? So many obstacles stood in the way, littering the path between there and here. Looming largest of all, like those boulders by the creek, was the fact that he wouldn't confide in her. Wouldn't talk about anything deeper than his work. And second to that were Susanna's feelings toward him. She wanted him gone, and Rachel couldn't see her reconciling herself to the opposite anytime soon. Then there was his work— he wasn't really a carpenter, or even a hired man. He was a cowboy, born and bred, a loner and a wanderer, answerable only to *Gott*.

She'd put herself in a real pickle. She might not be able to find that room in her heart anymore. But only because she'd opened the doors of her home and family to Luke Hertzler ... and it was getting more and more difficult to endure his walking away.

Thursday, May 12

No sooner had Willard Zook dropped off his gas-powered cultivator and departed in the buggy to take the twins to school, the Miller buggy rolled into the Inn's little parking lot and Reuben and Naomi climbed out.

Luke had been pretty sure there would be some kind of reaction from Rachel's relatives over the gift of the land. It might be kind of entertaining to see how she handled it, but at the moment she seemed to be staving it off by giving them the tour. All the windows were open to let in the warm morning, and from out in the yard he could hear their excited progress through the house. He could even hear Susanna's voice, which was a blessing. At least she was speaking to her aunt and uncle, if no one else.

But Susanna was not a problem he could solve just at the moment. Now that the hen and her chicks were safe in their new home, his job this morning was to get started on Rachel's vegetable garden. Like the old barn site, something had been here once, in the level stretch to one side of the parking lot, maybe fifty years ago, but it was all grown over in weeds and hay now. He drove in wooden stakes at the four corners of the large plot, then ran binder twine from one to the next to form a rectangle of the size she wanted.

He was tying the string to the final stake when he saw Reuben crossing the grass toward him, holding a pair of orange mugs from the set Rachel favored.

"Time for a coffee break," his old friend greeted him. He handed him a mug, which Luke saw had been doctored in just the way he liked. Rachel never missed a thing.

"*Denki*. I haven't really got to work yet. But I'll take you up on it."

"The soil here is *gut*, what with the creek drainage," Reuben observed, pushing his hat further up with one finger as he sipped. "She should have a fair crop, even with our short season. Naomi's putting in hers this week, too. Think you'll get it done by Sunday?"

"Cut and cultivated, at least, with Will's tiller," Luke said. "Don't know about planted. That's Rachel's department."

"That kitchen patio sure looks different from the last time I saw it. Where did you learn to lay bricks like that?"

Luke shrugged. "You know how it is. Every outfit you work for, you learn something."

"I don't know, as it happens—I've only ever worked on the Circle M."

"And I bet a year never goes by that you don't learn something new."

Reuben nodded. "True enough. I learned something new yesterday, in fact. Did you know about this idea of Rachel's?"

"I did," Luke said briefly. "She talked it over with Will and Zeke in my hearing. She wanted to make sure they understood her thinking, especially if they had plans for that hay field."

"Which they don't seem to?"

"*Neh.* They're pretty happy about the plan, I think. Your *Dochsder* and Noah King will be a *gut* addition—right in the middle of two districts, handy to both for carpentry. He should find some customers among the *Englisch* folks in town, too, along with the ranchers and the Amish."

Reuben looked at him, clearly surprised. "Hadn't thought of it that way, but you're right. I feel odd about them accepting such a valuable gift, for sure and certain, but I suppose my opinions don't hold much water."

"The way Rachel looks at it, and what she told Noah yesterday, is that his work is just as valuable. I hardly recognize this place anymore, he's put so much work into it. I think it's a fair trade, considering what she might get if she was to sell such a funny-shaped piece of dirt. Noah at least will be able to put it to *gut* use. Make it more productive than hay."

"That he will. It was all they could talk about last night." Thoughtfully, Reuben sipped his coffee. "You and Rachel getting used to talking things over these days?"

Reuben's tone was casual, but Luke understood the feeling behind it. "Some things. Mostly about the punch list."

"I understand there was a dust-up about a long-lost letter from my brother."

There was no point asking how he knew. Willard, probably, though Reuben likely wouldn't say even if Luke did ask. "*Ja*. It was addressed to me and never sent. Some busybody relative we both know saw something between me and Rachel thirty years ago and felt he had to confide it to Marlon." He tilted his head toward the house. "All the *Kinner* know about it, but it's hit Susanna the hardest. I guess she was pretty close to her *dat*."

"And a letter to you from my brother so long ago is somehow that *Maedscher*'s business?"

"She didn't know what it was. Found it in one of his books. She just saw Marlon's handwriting and opened it. Read it. Learned a thing or two about me and her mother. And it hasn't been the same between the two of them since." He paused, and finally decided that the words crowding his tongue ought to be released, for good or ill. "To tell the truth, Reuben, it disturbs me. I feel as though my being here is making the upset worse."

Under the brim of his hat, Reuben's greenish-hazel eyes were puzzled. "How can she make a fuss about something that happened long before she was born?"

"It's hard to explain. Rachel and I were seeing each other at the same time as she was seeing your brother. Marlon proposed, she made her choice, and we said good-bye. Life went on, my family moved away, and I met Eva." For once, his wife's name didn't cause a panic attack. Talking to Reuben was like that—like talking to a weathered tree that kept its own counsel, or a horse that had heard just about everything. "But to Susanna, I s'pose it looks like we're aiming to warm up cold soup."

"Are you?"

Luke gave a rueful smile at the hint of surprise in his tone. "Rachel's a fine woman. Capable. Faithful. And easy on the eyes, in some ways even more than she used to be. Any man would want to. Except this particular one has seen too much water under the bridge. She doesn't need to deal with all that."

"Have you talked with her about … all that?"

He shook his head. "No one needs that burden. Maybe I would have talked to Marlon, if he were still alive."

"Well, I have to say, whether you and Rachel have opened the subject or not, the Amish grapevine has been pretty exercised about the possibility of that soup."

With a sinking sensation in his belly, Luke wondered if that had anything to do with Susanna's attitude. "People say we're courting?"

"That's the long and the short of it. Without, you know, having any real facts to base it on."

Luke sighed. "Other than *she's a widow, he's a widower.* Therefore we're meant for each other."

"I'm sure you might have thought so thirty years ago." Reuben flicked a glance at him. "Along with that nameless relative, I noticed a thing or two back then. Others may have, too."

"But not Marlon."

Reuben shook his head, half a smile tilting up one corner of his lips. "He never noticed anything except Rachel."

Neither had Luke. It had taken years to get over her. Years until he had been able to care for and appreciate Eva in the way she deserved.

"What do you think?" he asked Reuben. "Would it be better for me to move on?"

"If you did, nothing would change. Susanna would still feel aggrieved, Rachel would still feel the brunt of it, and you'd be on the other side of the valley without a way to help either one."

"Trust you to see the big picture."

Reuben shrugged. "If it were me, and we were talking about Naomi and one of the twins, I wouldn't leave. I'd find a way to make it right."

"What if ... what if the gas under that soup accidentally got turned on?"

"Accidents are for icy roads and farm equipment, Luke," Reuben said. "It's hard to be accidental with that kind of soup." After a moment, he went on, "But if you did decide that it was best to move on, I heard this week that Josiah Keim is looking for a foreman. Seems theirs has decided to retire and move to where his kids are. He's *Englisch*. *Gut* to have an Amishman in that position."

Reuben squeezed his shoulder, collected the coffee mugs, and made his way back toward the house. Leaving Luke trying to figure out whether Reuben really meant for him to inquire about the Keim job, or stay here and finish the one he had.

No matter what that might mean.

﹩ 17 ﹪

WHEN THE CELL phone rang late that afternoon, it startled Rachel so that she barely managed to get both loaves of bread in the oven before she dropped them.

What's that sound? was written plainly on Susanna's face. Then her daughter's expression cleared. "It's the phone. Who's going to get it?"

It was practically the first thing she'd said to Rachel since the day before yesterday. "You," she said. "You're closest."

Susanna hurried into Rachel's room and the next moment, sounded completely composed as she said, "Wild Rose Amish Inn, Susanna speaking. Oh, hi, Alison ... is it really? You did? Oh, my goodness, when?"

Rachel couldn't help herself. She went to the bedroom doorway as Susanna sat and, for the first time, opened the day planner that she'd found at the variety store to put their bookings in.

"Niedermayr, coming in Thursday night the twenty-sixth, leaving the thirty-first. That's the long weekend. How many? Got it." She looked over her shoulder at the doorway, saw

Rachel there, and couldn't seem to help a grin. "All right, and the other one? Johnson, party of four?"

"Adults or children?" Rachel hissed.

"Adults or children? Oh, fishermen. Those are coming opening day—no, our opening day, not the river—and staying until the twenty-eighth. Got it. Oh, this is so exciting! Mamm will be thrilled." She was silent for a long while, listening. "Yes, I'll tell her. Thanks so much, Alison."

She disconnected and practically clapped her hands. Then she double-checked what she'd written in the planner before she met her mother's gaze. "Alison said she got the website finished the same night as she was here, and put it on a bunch of those advertising sites, and within a day had two reservations in the booking system."

"We have a booking system?"

Susanna waved her hands. "I guess we do. She says it's paid in advance so we don't have to deal with credit cards and the internet and all that. And she says if we have drop-ins, to take cash only, or a check from a Montana resident only."

"That makes it simple." Rachel crossed the room to gaze at the two entries in Susanna's neat handwriting. "It's really real," she said. "Do you feel ready?"

"I think so, *ja*. My heart is beating pretty fast though—and it was only Alison."

"Mine is, too. Just think, by next month we'll be old hands at this, up to our ears in laundry."

"The laundry service will, anyway," Susanna said. "Imagine us trying to turn over eight guest beds and two bathrooms every other day with our gas-driven washer. It's hard enough keeping the boys in clean sheets once a week."

Rachel marveled at how easy she seemed to be. The need to speak welled up in Rachel's chest. "*Dochsder*, have you given any more thought to what I said to you the other night? About forgiveness?" She sat on the edge of her bed.

Susanna put the pencil down and turned in the chair. "I've been thinking, *ja*. I've also noticed Luke is keeping his distance." She lowered her head. "I suppose I shouldn't let the Amish grapevine get me all twisted up."

The tension in Rachel's chest uncoiled a little. Best not to mention that it was hardly fair to expect a man keep his distance when he hadn't done anything wrong. "It's not easy sometimes."

"Maybe this news about giving the parcel to Noah and Rebecca will give everybody something else to talk about."

"I expect so, starting with her parents yesterday."

Susanna smiled with her lips, though her eyes were troubled. "I do forgive you, Mamm. If you forgive me for speaking to you that way. And if you'll tell me for true that you were faithful to Dat all the time you were married."

Something else Rachel would never mention—that while of course she had been physically faithful, there had still been that secret room and its forbidden contents. "I tell you so for true, *Liewi*. I loved your father, and he loved me. The kind of love that sees a woman through, no matter how hard life gets."

Susanna nodded, and when she lifted her head, a real smile trembled on her lips. Rachel pushed away the thought that even now, she couldn't tell her daughter the truth. But maybe that was between her and the Lord. Between her and Susanna now, there was only relief and a big hug.

Her sons came home from work not long afterward, and dinner talk was all about their very first bookings. The afternoons were long enough now that she could look out the keeping room window and see Luke still out there past the parking lot, walking slowly up and down with the cultivator, bumping over the ground, turning under the wildflowers and hay within their boundaries of string. She didn't like to look on them as weeds. A weed was just a plant on the inside that should be on the outside.

He turned at the end of the row, and began in the other direction. A woman with a heart would invite him to stay for supper.

But a woman who had just been given the gift of forgiveness was not about to do anything that would cause that gift to be rescinded. She wasn't sure what hurt the most—that she had kept a tiny part of the truth from Susanna, or that she was allowing her daughter to affect the way she treated Luke. Wasn't part of a Christian's walk to be open and honest with those around her? Why did it have to come down to a choice between her relationship with Susanna and her relationship with Luke?

Not that she and he really had a relationship. But a friendship of many years' standing was pretty close, wasn't it? Did Susanna really expect her to give that up for the sake of peace?

Communion Sunday

In the Siksika Valley, the *Gross Gmay*—the "big church," or Communion—began at eight and usually concluded by four in the afternoon. The preceding weeks, Luke thought, had been preparing him for today, from the sermons on New Life to the *Ordnungs Gmay* two weeks ago, to the time of fasting the previous Sunday. All these observances, small and great, led up to today.

In his freshly laundered white shirt, black weskit, and black pants, he took his place on the bench on the men's side in the Eicher family's machine shed beside Willard and Hezekiah.

This morning he was grateful and glad that matters had been cleared up between himself and Zeke. Luke had forgiven him without hesitation, and it seemed that between the two of them now there existed a peace, an ease, that had not been there in the weeks since he'd arrived. Truly, *Gott*'s wisdom was a wide and *wunderbaar* thing.

They sang an opening hymn, then of course the *Loblied,* then two more hymns while the ministers were in the *Abrot*, or ministers' council before the sermons began. During the last hymn, the ministers filed back into the room. Little Joe cleared his throat and began the *Forstellung*, or the introduction of what would be spoken of today. Here, as in Luke's old church in Wisconsin, the ministers followed what he'd often heard called the "Golden Path"—tracing Communion from the patriarchs, to the prophecies, to the very life and death of Christ in the New Testament.

He and the Zook brothers sat on the backless bench, approaching *der Herr* together in spirit. As a child, the two morning sermons following the *Forstellung*—the *Anfang*, or beginning, and the *Altvater*, the patriarchs—had seemed so long that he'd been convinced *der Herr* had a finger on the sun, preventing its forward movement. But today, when Willard shifted and indicated they might step outside to fetch the basket he'd packed, Luke found that the sun had reached its meridian almost before he expected it.

Surely the Lord would understand if, just as in his *Rumspringe* days, some of that time had been spent in covertly watching Rachel on the women's side. Not much, mind, but some.

Lunch was sandwiches of thinly sliced pork from the roast the previous night, thick with lettuce and sliced mushrooms and horseradish. Dried apple hand pies and a Thermos flask of coffee rounded out the meal, and they resumed their seats quietly as other families came and went to the tables set up outside. Rachel's family was going out in a group as they came in. Luke would have been sorry not to eat together, except that the meal was not for visiting, but for sustaining the body through the next part of the day.

Little Joe, it seemed, was one of those observant bishops who timed the *Leide*, the sermon of Christ's suffering on the cross, to conclude at the hour when tradition held he had died —the third hour, or three o'clock. Little Joe was a painter of words; there was more than one pair of eyes lowered with grief for the Savior, the perfect one who had died a criminal's death for the sakes of those who believed on Him. The ministers broke the loaf that had been sitting on a table close by, and carried it to each side. After a prayer and more Scripture, they poured the wine into a single cup from which each one would sip, and they sang the communion hymn.

> *Merst aus mit Fleiß, ein Himmelspeiß*
> *Ist uns von Gott gegeben,*
> *Durch Jesum Christ, welcher da ist*
> *Gott's Wort, vernimm mich eben.*
> *Denselben hat im Anfang Gott*
> *Den Vätern thun verheissen,*
> *Zur Seligfeit und we'ger Freud,*
> *Darin'n thät er es Ieisten.*

> *Listen diligently, the bread of heaven*
> *Is to us by God given,*
> *Through Jesus Christ, who there is*
> *God's word, to which I beg you'll listen.*
> *Even He has God in the beginning*

Promised to the fathers of old,
With salvation and eternal joy,
Completes God's will foretold.

When they fell silent, Little Joe said, "We remember Christ's sacrifice as we take these emblems of His body, broken for us, and His blood, shed for our sins. And we remember that without the breaking and grinding of the wheat, so that no individual grain can be distinguished any more, there can be no bread. Without the crushing of the grape, and the blending of the juice from each one, there can be no wine. If even one grape or grain of wheat remains whole, it is separate from the others, and misses out both on fellowship and fulfilling its own purpose."

Luke took a sip of the wine, as the minister brought it to him in his turn. *Help me to fit in here, Lord, like these crushed grapes. And if it's Your will that I move on again, let it be with Your guidance and not by my own will. I put myself in Your hands.*

Then came the second of the three important ceremonies: the foot washing.

But instead of simply turning to the next person on the bench, Luke found that the tradition had changed under Little Joe's tenure. Now every other row turned to the one behind, so that there was one older person and one younger. Ach, Joe was wise. For washing the feet of your buddy bunch—your friends of the same age beside you on the bench—was solemn, all right, but it wasn't really an act of *Gelassenheit* or joyful submission. But for a young man to wash Luke's feet, or a man of Luke's age to wash the feet of one of the elderly—now, that was service. The same went on the women's side. The hymn he'd always associated with the foot washing began as the ministers brought out tubs of warm water and towels. It seemed to Luke that to sing as you served another was a metaphor for how God wanted the *Gmay* to live in community with each other.

Daniel Miller, who was seated behind him, poured water from his cupped hands three times over Luke's bare feet, signifying the Trinity, and dried them with the towel. Luke did the same for Daniel. When they had put on their socks and boots once more, Luke quietly said the traditional words, "The Lord be with us," before he gave Daniel the kiss of peace.

"Amen to peace," Daniel murmured, and offered the kiss in return.

They resumed their places, each symbolizing to the other his commitment to the *Gmay*. And wasn't that God's plan, Luke thought as he picked up the words of the hymn and began to sing once more. If each member had committed him or herself to an individual today, then one at a time, the entire *Gmay* became committed to fellowship.

The final ceremony of the day affirmed it, as, still singing, the members filed past a plain wooden box with a hinged lid and a slot in the top. The giving of alms on Communion Sunday was the only time Luke had seen any kind of collection taken as part of the service. He slid a couple of bills into the slot under cover of his palm, for it would be wrong to let anyone see the amount. Those who could not give much would be ashamed, and those who could afford more might be tempted to pride. Keeping it discreet saved them from that and kept the focus on its purpose, because the *gut Gott* only knew which of them might need alms in the six months to come.

With the words of the hymn still ringing in his ears, he followed Willard and Hezekiah outside. Today, there would be no visiting and volleyball games for the *Youngie* before an evening spent singing. Today was sacred to the life and death of Christ. People greeted each other, of course, and then collected their *Kinner* and elderly relatives while the boys went to catch the family's horses for the ride home.

Since the Zook brothers were related to Rachel, it would not be unusual if he tagged along with them to greet her and her family. They saw each other every day, after all. But as he shook hands with her sons and ruffled the hair of little Benny, Susanna offered her hand, too.

"*Guder owed*, Luke," she said. She didn't smile, but the greeting was enough for him.

"*Guder owed*." He hoped his handshake communicated friendliness along with firmness.

What had brought about this change? He hadn't seen hide nor hair of the girl in a couple of days, and now she had been the one to offer her hand first. But *der Herr* moved in mysterious ways, and maybe He had been moving in Susanna's heart.

Even so, he didn't dare hold Rachel's hand any longer than he'd gripped those of her sons. But to his surprise, she kept her hand in his for just one second past politeness. Just long enough to squeeze it and let it go. Her lashes flicked up and down, quick as a bird's wing in flight. Just long enough for him to see some warmth—some secret happiness—he hadn't seen there before. Or at least, not since they'd been reckless kids together. Just a flash—not long enough to be noticeable by anyone else. But enough to make him feel like an earthquake had just ceased under his feet, leaving the earth quiet once more, but completely changed.

All the way home with the Zooks, he was unable to speak except for one-word, distracted answers. After their pick-up supper, he took refuge in his room. Let them believe he was tired out after the day. He changed out of his church clothes and into his work jeans and old chambray shirt. Then he lay on the bed, wondering if he'd imagined it all—handshake, glance, even the single look they'd exchanged as they'd passed each other at the door at lunchtime.

She was a friend, that was all. Friends looked at each other. Friends shook hands. She was probably happy about Susanna's change of heart.

More than that has changed and I need to know what.

The evening breeze puffed under the sash of the half-open window, scented with the grass Will had mowed yesterday. From somewhere close by, a robin trilled a good night, liquid notes pouring into the dusk. It seemed to call him. Suddenly he couldn't bear to be inside another minute—he had to be outdoors in the evening air, compelled by an urgency that he didn't understand, but could not deny.

He slid his feet into his boots and slipped out the front door his hosts never used. In five minutes he had crossed Noah and Rebecca's land and found the footpath by the chuckling creek. It ran along beside him, all the way to the Inn ... and Rachel.

Supper at the Inn that evening had been a quiet meal. The twins were exhausted after the long day attempting to sit still, and even her sons and Susanna didn't have much to say for themselves as they ate their noodle soup and dipped tortilla chips in salsa and *chile con queso* made from *gut* Zook cheese. Maybe they had been hoping there would be a singing after the Communion services, or an invitation to someone's home. But it seemed that now, as when she was growing up here, the *Gmay* still kept the solemnity of the day right through until bedtime. No buggies came to visit from the Circle M, no young folk crossed the bridge from Mountain Home.

Rachel supposed she should be thankful. Sunday was supposed to be a day of rest, but many times it didn't feel that way. Some folks, like Susanna and Gideon, found being with people raised their spirits and gave them energy. Rachel sometimes did, but more often she was like Tobias and Seth, who refreshed themselves by being quiet with only a few, or reading, building a puzzle, or going for a walk in the evening dusk.

This was the first time since they'd moved here that she

hadn't felt the faraway breath of the glacier in the evening air. Tonight, after a day of welcome sunshine, it actually felt as though summer was waiting at the gate, impatient to be let in. She followed a sweet scent over to their own gate, and found that the wild roses had burst into bloom while they'd been occupied with the events of the day.

Delighted, she buried her nose in a big cluster of pink blossoms and breathed. "What *gut* timing you have," she told the thick hedge of bushes that crowded the split rail fence. "Our first guests come at the end of the week, and you'll all be here to welcome them. I must remember to dig up a few of you for our front steps."

"Who are you talking to?" came a quiet, amused voice from the other side of the gate. A familiar voice. One she knew as well as those of her children. Only her children's voices didn't jolt her heart in quite this way, or make her breath come a little faster.

"The roses." She opened the gate and he slipped through. "I was welcoming them, the way they're going to welcome our guests in a few days."

As though by mutual consent, they walked slowly in the direction of what would soon be her garden. Away from the house.

"Quite a day today," he said.

"It's been a long while since I've had a Communion Sunday," she said, counting back to when it had last been for them. "Last spring, we were down to two families and had already lost a minister. I felt sorry for two men having to bear the load of preaching instead of four. And the singing—my goodness. It was all we could do to carry the tunes. By fall, the deacon and his family had gone, and there only the bishop. He did his best, but even with Tobias's help, the services were over by one o'clock, like an ordinary church Sunday."

"The twins probably appreciated that. They were well behaved today."

"Tobias let me have them for the afternoon preaching. Luckily they were sleepy after lunch."

They fell silent, idly walking the perimeter of the rumpled, tilled soil. It would need to be raked and furrowed before planting, but the hard work was done.

"I was—" he began.

"I heard—" She laughed at herself. "You first."

"I was happy that Susanna seemed willing to speak after church. I hoped she might be coming around. To accept my being here."

She was grateful that his perception had saved her explanations. "She's forgiven me."

His sigh was audible. "I'm glad. Though after thirty years, it's hard for me to understand what there is to forgive. Heaven knows we've paid for our sins." He looked off toward the belt of trees, dark against the gentle slope. "At least, I have. I can't speak for you, of course."

"Your sins were no greater than mine. It grieves me, Luke, so much. What you've had to go through—"

For a moment, she thought she'd gone too far, her uncontrolled tongue alluding to his family again. She expected him to turn and disappear into the rapidly falling darkness as suddenly as he'd appeared out of it.

But he didn't. Instead, he stood firm, gazing out over the field. "I've never talked about it. With anyone."

She dared to speak up, half afraid she'd frighten him off, a deer venturing out of the woods for the first time. "We've always been able to talk to one another."

"*Ja*, we have, and there was many a time I was grateful for it. Each hour you spent listening to me moan about how hard it was living under Dat's iron hand will be accounted to you for righteousness, I'm pretty sure."

"Yet you moved to Wisconsin to help him on the farm."

"It wasn't easy. But after—" He stopped. "It was the right thing to do, in the end. It led me to Eva. *Gott's* hand was clearly at work." When she didn't speak, he went on, "I never thought I was good enough for her. Certainly not on our wedding day, when I said my vows to her with you still in my heart."

"I did the same," she whispered. "But after Tobias was born, I closed the door on that secret room where you lived, and gave my heart without reservation to Marlon."

He nodded, which she sensed more than saw, since nearly all the light was gone. "Funny how our lives have run in parallel that way. Or maybe it's just what happens when you choose to love the one *Gott* has led you to ... instead of looking back."

"Maybe."

"Marlon deserved you. More than Eva deserved me. At least you weren't responsible for his death."

Her heart gave another jolt. Was he on the verge of speaking about those dark days, here in the dusk?

"The cancer was *Gott's wille*," she said. "Though I've wished many a time that I'd paid more attention. That I'd seen the signs. By the time I finally did, and we went to a doctor, it was too late."

"Don't blame yourself, Rachel. Marlon didn't want to burden you, I suspect. Just like I don't want to burden you with my ... memories."

"Grossmammi used to say that sharing a burden halves its weight."

"Is that how the proverb goes? I think it's *marriage halves our griefs and doubles our joys*, isn't it?"

"You can still share your burden with me. You may find Grossmammi's proverb is true, even if we're not married."

Even if we're not married.

The words seemed to hang in the air like the moisture just before the dew falls.

He cleared his throat. "We were taking the *Boppli* to the doctor for her six-month checkup. The *Kinner* were supposed to go to a neighbor, but somehow they talked us into letting them come—I think Silas was hoping we'd go to the feed store afterward. It was his favorite place in town. So I was frustrated that I wouldn't get the chance to talk to Eva. We'd been fighting, you see. She wanted to break the lease on the farm and go back to Oak Hill, Pennsylvania, like her parents did. I was determined to stay, to make a success of our place in Wisconsin if it was the last thing I did. Too many years of watching Dat struggle with the land in Montana gave me what I thought were some *gut* ideas about how to farm properly. So many nights studying, and reading books. Talking to other farmers at the co-op." He paused. "Talking to her, trying to convince her to give it another year."

"Oak Hill? Isn't that near Whinburg Township?"

"*Ja.* I'd been there, but Lancaster County doesn't suit me. I'm a westerner for good and all, I guess. It's too tame out there, after two hundred years of Amish discipline and management. Too orderly and prosperous. Not like Wisconsin."

She chuckled. "Or Montana. People sometimes come here thinking they can manage it. Discipline it. But nobody gets the upper hand with Montana."

"My father sure didn't. Anyway, we left our place in the

buggy just as the sun was coming up. Eva said something—I don't even remember what—but I know I was upset. My mind not on my driving. The sun glared right in my eyes as I made that left turn onto the county road. I never even saw that big dually pickup."

Rachel gasped, the horror of that moment a dreadful picture in her mind's eye.

"To this day I don't remember it. I just remember a horrible scream, whether outside or inside the buggy, I don't know. Afterward, the policeman told me I'd been thrown out of the buggy, all the way across the two lanes of the road and into the ditch. The truck hit Eva's side. She and the *Boppli* were killed instantly. By the time I regained consciousness in the hospital, *Gott* had gathered Silas and Jessie home to Himself as well. As for the horse ... well, they put it down on the spot."

"And the driver of the truck?"

"Poor man. He didn't see me, either, because our lane had trees on either side of the entrance and he wasn't familiar with the road. He had some injury from the air bag, but he survived. He—he paid my hospital bills. A decent man. They investigated, and concluded that he hadn't been speeding, and I'd been blinded by the sun when I made that turn." He took a deep, shuddering breath. "The truth is, I was blinded by anger and impatience. If I'd just waited two more seconds—" He bowed his head in shame. "They said it wasn't my fault, but I know in my heart it was."

His voice trembled, and his chest hitched in a sob like the first gust of a storm.

Rachel's heart broke. "Oh Luke, to have carried this burden all these years." She slid her arms around him and hugged him tight—so tight that she felt the moment when the storm hit and he gave himself up to grief. It might have been the first time he'd allowed himself to do so. She didn't know. All she knew was that if she let him go, if she stepped away, he'd never open up to her again. So she held him, and murmured words of comfort, and at last felt his arms go around her the way a man clings to a tree in a tornado.

She hadn't been held by a man since Marlon died. And oh, it was a battle to remember that she was supposed to be offering comfort, not breathing in the scent of clean cotton and skin warmed by emotion. Not supposed to be rubbing his back this way, feeling the hard muscle under his shirt instead of soothing him the way she would a weeping child.

Luke Hertzler was no child, nor the young man he had been, either. He was different and yet the same. Her old friend, and yet only a couple of weeks ago he had been a stranger. The man she had begun to love, and yet the man she had given up.

When at last the storm blew itself out, he made a hesitant motion to withdraw. She pulled a handkerchief from her sleeve and offered it to him. He blew his nose and mopped his face and such homely actions brought her back to herself.

No thoughts like those for you, my girl. He's just got done baring his soul to you and what are you doing? Glorying in the flesh. You should be ashamed of yourself.

Luke dragged in a breath as though he'd been under water. Maybe he had. But did he know now that he had friends to pull him out? That he wasn't going to drown?

"Bischt du okay?" she murmured, tucking the handkerchief away.

"I feel as weak as one of those little chicks in the coop," he said, with a breath of a laugh. *"Denki.* For your patience. And your comfort. I feel … strange."

"Lighter?" she asked.

Now he was able to look into her face, though she couldn't see much more than the outline of his eyes and jaw against the stars. "Maybe," he said on a note of realization. "You don't condemn me?"

"I think you've been living the life of a condemned man since that morning," she said honestly. "I think *der Herr* might have guided you home again to begin the life of a free man. Not the kind of free that makes you wander from one state to another. But the kind that leaves you free to feel again. To start over ... right here ... where you started." She tilted her head to gaze up at the sky. "To see the stars, and marvel at the hand that put them there. To look at a place and call it home, not just a job."

"Ach, Rachel," he murmured. "Don't you know that wherever I go, you are my home?"

She barely had time to draw in a breath of surprise when his arms went around her this time. And not because he needed comfort. Because he needed *her*.

His mouth came down on hers, finding it unerringly, fitting together just as they always had, but after thirty years, strange and new. She curled her fingers in his shirt, but whether it was to pull him closer or push him away, she would never know.

Because at that moment, a blinding glare shone in her eyes. And somebody shrieked, *"Mamm!"*

🦋 19 🦋

RUNNING footsteps took off in the direction of the house and, still trying to gather her wits, Rachel realized they had been interrupted by Susanna, holding a flashlight.

"*Ach, neh*," she sighed. "I'd better go in."

"I'll come with you."

"*Neh*, Luke. I'll talk to her another time, when she's not so upset."

"We are in this together. We'll talk to her together."

"If she lets us."

"From where I stand, she's living under your roof. You're the one who tells her what's what, *nix*? Not the other way around."

He had a point. Then again— "You don't know Susanna like I do."

"That's true. But even the bishop would agree we've done nothing wrong."

The bishop and the word buzzing along the grapevine was one thing. They would only see a courtship from the outside. But Rachel knew Susanna already suspected she'd been

196

emotionally unfaithful to her father, and with this very man. At the same time, Rachel couldn't help but appreciate Luke's determination to stand at her side. He could have faded off into the darkness. But once again, he hadn't.

"All right. Gird your loins."

They found Susanna in the family parlor, clearly having just told all three of her brothers the shocking details. At least the twins were already in bed asleep—Rachel would not have wanted them to hear this.

Gideon's lips were already twitching, and at the sight of her and Luke in the doorway between the family parlor and the kitchen, he laughed out loud. "Here they are, the guilty pair themselves. Honestly, Mamm, don't you know you're supposed to keep a courtship quiet? Any of the *Youngie* could tell you that."

"This is not funny!" Susanna snapped.

"*Schweschder*, it's you who's funny. What an old lady you are! So shocked at people kissing. What are you going to do when someone tries to kiss *you*?"

Susanna turned scarlet. "Don't you make fun of me. It's not about me. It's about our mother cheating on our father with that man!" She pointed a shaking finger at Luke.

"In case you missed it, *Schweschder*, our father has been dead for nearly six years." Seth was pale, and clearly uncomfortable at the raised voices.

"Oh, don't be a child." Her voice was a lash. "I mean cheating on Dat in her heart while she was married."

"Will someone who was actually there at the time care to speak?" Luke asked mildly.

"*Ja*, I will," Rachel said. It was time for her to take control of this ugly situation before the words got so sharp the wounds they left wouldn't heal.

"You already lied to me once—" Susanna began.

"Susanna, be silent."

"But you're just going to—"

"I said, be silent!"

Her daughter clamped her lips together, but fire and brimstone snapped in her eyes. She may as well have screamed a second time, for all the submission she was displaying.

"Tobias will agree with me when I say that when someone you love is removed from your life, you don't simply stop loving them. It takes time—sometimes years—for that love to ... change. To become less grief and more sweetness. Would you say that was true, *mei Sohn?*"

Tobias nodded. "Sometimes it never changes."

"And sometimes it changes into warmth and welcome, that will allow new love to enter in," Luke said quietly.

Rachel went on, "I will confess to you all that when I married your father, I loved him—but at the same time, I was in love with Luke. *Love* and *in love* are two different things. But it took time for love to grow on one side and the other to fade. You all know that your father was aware of my feelings. You've read his letter to Luke. And yet, he loved me so much that he was willing to wait until my heart was whole again. Wholly his. And when it was, our marriage became deeper and richer."

"Our father was a *gut Mann*," Tobias said, his voice husky. "We all know that your marriage was happy, Mamm."

"Because it was wholehearted," Rachel said.

"What about *your* marriage?" Susanna dared to ask Luke. "Can you say the same?"

Seth looked shocked at her tone. With all her strength, Rachel held back a torrent of sharp words, as protective as a barbed-wire fence.

"Your mother and I were just talking about that, outside," he said quietly.

Rachel blessed him for not taking offense. Any other man would have. She had.

"My experience was much the same," he went on. "I was *in love* with your mother, but she *loved* your father. It was the right choice, though it was hard for me to see it at the time. But *Gott* led me to Eva, and I found it was possible to love in the way that lasts. With a whole heart. To have a family and rejoice at seeing her in the faces, the eyes of our *Kinner.*"

No one in the room but Rachel knew what it cost him to speak Eva's name. To speak of his children. It was an act of bravery—and the next step on the road to healing.

In the silence, Rachel could also see Susanna's struggle. It was almost as though she believed she had to take her father's part—to say for him the things he had not said in his letter. But how could that be? How could she take that upon herself —to open a book that *Gott* had closed with Marlon's death— and be angry with what was written there?

The old sofa creaked as Tobias rose. "I don't know about anyone else, but as the only other person in this room who has lost his wife, I can say from my heart that if you are thinking of courting my mother, Luke, then for what it's worth, you have my blessing."

Luke's chin trembled for just a moment before he grasped Tobias's hand. "It's worth a great deal," he said hoarsely.

Wordlessly, Gideon and Seth rose to shake his hand, too. Gideon even added a brief hug.

Luke's emotion was clear on his face as his gaze moved to Susanna, who had not moved. They stood in a ragged circle, but somehow she seemed to be set apart. The stiffness in her body, maybe. The absence of peace.

"I'll say *guder nacht* now," she said, and walked out of the room. A moment later, her bedroom door closed with such quiet care it might as well have been a slam.

Monday, May 16

Four days left before the Inn was to open, and Rachel wondered what shape they'd be in to welcome guests. What kind of spirit would be in this house. How could she have gone from the peace and spiritual rejuvenation of Communion to that kiss with Luke to hearing words hurled in anger among her *Kinner*—all within the space of a couple of hours?

Human nature, that was how.

Rachel gathered up her church clothes and added them to her sons' pile in the laundry basket. Monday was wash day in many Amish communities, and the Siksika was no exception. Basket on her hip, she knocked on her daughter's door and spoke through the panel. "Susanna, bring your laundry when you come out to start breakfast."

She got no answer, but that wasn't surprising. Ah well. She'd try again to talk to her—or better yet, maybe she'd ask Tobias to have a quiet heart-to-heart. Susanna had always looked up to her eldest brother, and his experience with the joy and the heartbreak of love could still be a blessing to her.

Downstairs, Rachel started the gas-powered engine that drove the washing machine, then separated the clothes and put in the whites. Like every Amish woman she knew, she and Susanna washed and starched their *Kapps* by hand—maybe she'd do that for her today. When she climbed the stairs to the kitchen, Seth and Gideon had their coffee and were leaning on the counter, talking over plans for the day. She could hear

Tobias down the hall, waking the twins for breakfast and school.

No Susanna.

Well, being angry with her was one thing, but letting her hardworking brothers wait for their breakfast was quite another. Rachel marched down the hall and knocked on her door again. "Susanna? *Kumm mit*, now. It's time to start breakfast or the *Kinner* will be late for school."

Silence. Well, she'd told her last night to be silent, so maybe she was making a point of taking her at her word.

"Susanna?" Rachel opened the door.

The bed was neatly made. Dresses with their matching capes and aprons hung in the closet. One hanger was bare, and a pair of shoes was missing. So were her sweater and her second *Kapp* —the first hung on its peg by its strings. Well, she hadn't been in the basement. Maybe she was out communing with the chicks.

While Rachel got the eggs and bacon out, she sent Seth outside to check. He came back shaking his head. "Not there, Mamm."

She turned from the frying pan. "For pity's sake. It's five in the morning. Where could she be?"

"Almost anywhere," Seth said, taking the spatula and nudging her out of the way so he could turn the bacon. "Let's get breakfast on the table, and by then maybe she'll have come back."

Gideon took plates down and began to set the table. "Without a horse and buggy, she can't have gone far. I'll sure be glad when our barn is built and we can keep animals here like normal people."

Rachel was at a loss, but it was *gut* advice. No point panicking on an empty stomach.

After breakfast, she cleared the table while the bustle of people getting ready to go to work and school swung into action. In the midst of it, she somehow heard the still unfamiliar shrill of the cell phone. Goodness. She half hoped it was Alison giving her some information about their website. With everything going on, if it was a prospective guest she was sure to forget some important thing and mess up the booking.

She hurried into her bedroom and took the cell phone out of the middle drawer of the desk. "Wild Rose Amish Inn, Rachel speaking."

"Rachel, it's Naomi," her sister-in-law said. Her voice sounded peculiar, as though she were speaking with one hand over her mouth.

"Hallo," she said. "This is a first—a call from you on our new phone. Rebecca's not planning to come and collect the twins, is she?"

"It's not Rebecca," Naomi said tersely. "It's Susanna. Rachel, she's just walked five miles in the dark to get here and wants to know if she can stay. What do you want me to tell her? What on earth is going on?"

Circle M Ranch

Reuben Miller came into the kitchen, which was full of *Youngie* doing dishes and talking up a storm as usual. Naomi clicked off the cell phone looking winded. And pale. Wordlessly, she put it back in the cookie jar and gave him the look that said, *We need to talk right now.*

It was the kind of day that the *gut Gott* had created Montana for—the air warming as the sun lifted over the still snowy peaks of the Siksika Range—the wild roses and daisies blooming as hard as they could while they could. So with a word to his sons that he would catch up with them at the allotment, where they'd be checking the calves who had been turned out a couple of weeks ago, he took his wife's hand and, together, they climbed the track up to Mammi's orchard.

The only place close to the house where they could find some privacy.

The two of them had been coming here during moments of joy and sorrow for the length of their marriage. Mamm hadn't merely planted six apple trees, much to the amusement of the church. She'd proven wrong their predictions that the trees would fail, and created a sanctuary for her family for generations to come. Every time Reuben came here, he thanked *Gott* for his mother's foresight.

"Look—the apples have set." Naomi touched a little cluster of fruit, hard and barely the size of grapes, but full of potential. Then she sighed. "I'm afraid that you and I have started something that it seems *Gott* wants us to finish."

The story came spilling out, from Luke Hertzler's reappearance in the valley where they'd all grown up, to that unguarded conversation in the bedroom after Council Meeting, to a long lost letter, to their niece's unexpected appearance at breakfast this morning. Reuben found he had to sit down on the cut-out log bench conveniently located for this purpose, and Naomi settled beside him.

"Rachel thought that she and Susanna had cleared the air before *Gross Gmay*, but last night the worst happened."

"They had an argument?" Reuben asked.

"Worse than that—Susanna caught Rachel and Luke outside on the lawn. In the dark. *Kissing*."

Reuben couldn't help it. A whoop of laughter exploded out of him.

His darling *Fraa* glared at him, affronted. "It's not funny!"

"Oh, but it is. That was *not* what I expected you to say."

Her lips twitched. "All right. It is funny. Usually it's the other way around—parents surprising their *Kinner*. But Reuben, we have to be serious about this. Susanna has essentially run away from home, and Rachel is beside herself. She says Susanna got to be *gut* friends with Emily Kuepfer over Christmas. They've been corresponding, apparently, and Rachel is terrified that Susanna is going to find a way to Libby, get on a train, and never come back."

Was the girl capable of crossing the continent just to spite her mother? Well, it didn't matter. Rachel thought she was, and that was the important thing.

"What is she asking us to do?"

"Send her back, I suppose—they have a business opening in a couple of days. Though nobody is thinking about business this morning. Rachel says Susanna was close to her *dat*—that she feels somehow she has to take his part and hold her and Luke to account for seeing each other while she was also seeing Marlon."

"That sounds a little crazy, *nix*? This all happened more than a decade before she was born."

"Sure, but that's not the point. The point is, it's how she feels. Maybe that's why she came here. Because you're Marlon's brother. The closest she has to her father."

Reuben began to see the direction in which his wife's thoughts were taking her. And him. "You want me to have a talk with her."

"The more I think on it, the more I believe that's why she's here, even if maybe she doesn't know it. She could have gone to the Stolzfus house—or the Yoders—to get some space. They're only a couple of blocks away. But she walked five miles

THE AMISH COWBOY'S REFUGE

to come to us. Because you're her father's brother, and somewhere deep down, she needs you."

Reuben wasn't sure that his putting his oar in the water at
this late date would do any good, but if life with Rebecca and
Malena had taught him anything, it was that sometimes just
being available to listen was the best gift a father could give a
young woman.

"All right," he said. "I don't suppose she'd want to ride
fence while we have it out, would she?"

"No, *mei Liewe*," she said with a shake of the head. "I'll go
down and tell her you want to talk with her right here, where
all our important conversations seem to happen."

20

CIRCLE M RANCH

SUSANNA APPEARED in the mouth of the little box canyon, gazing around her with wondering eyes. It occurred to Reuben that in all their comings and goings since Christmas, she had never been up here.

He ambled over to where she was examining the newly set fruit. "Your grandmother planted this orchard," he said. "Everyone in church laughed at her—told her that with a three-month growing season, the trees would freeze and fail and she wouldn't even have firewood for her pains. But what they didn't know is there's a natural spring here, and the canyon faces south. It's sheltered from the worst of the storms. That tree there is a Lodi. It was your *dat*'s favorite. The pies Mamm would make from it! I can taste them even yet."

"Dat's favorite?" She touched the tree as though it, too, retained some connection with her father. "He did like an apple pie. I think the first time I ever baked something all on my own was a lopsided apple turnover for him."

"And he enjoyed every bite, I bet."

She smiled at the memory. "He sure did. Even if it was a little burned on the bottom."

"You're talking to the man who enjoys the cookies with the well-done bottoms," he said, sharing her smile. "Marlon and I had that in common." No time like the present to plunge his oar in. "Along with *Gott* blessing us in the wives He meant for us."

"I suppose you know what's been going on at our house."

"I have a little idea of my part in the whole *Uffrohr*. I'm sorry for that. Suppose you tell me your view on it."

She did, at length, with a voice that rose in indignation and fell in grief. The story wasn't much different from the one he had heard from Naomi, but the details of her shame over the district's gossip and the deep-seated protectiveness she held for her father's memory were new.

By the time she ran out of steam, they were both sitting on the log, and she looked exhausted. No wonder—that walk this morning would have taken a couple of hours, and now all this emotion on top of it.

After a moment, she said, "I don't know what to do. I've told my mother how I feel, and she ignores me."

"Does she?"

Susanna snorted. "Kissing Luke out there in the dark is ignoring me, *nix*?"

"Maybe at that moment she didn't have time to think about her *Kinner*."

"And isn't that just the way. She didn't think about Dat's feelings when she was busy kissing Luke thirty years ago, either."

"Marlon knew."

"I know. He wrote Luke a letter."

"So I understand. But I mean to say, he knew about it before Hezekiah told him."

Her whole being seemed to freeze. "How do you know that?"

He nudged her with his shoulder. "I'm his brother. He talked to me. Asked me what he should do."

"And what did you say?" Her gentian blue eyes, so like Rachel's, held his with an almost magnetic command, as though daring him to look away.

Which he did, turning his face to the morning sky for a moment and sending up a prayer for the right words. "I told him that *der Herr* had brought him and Rachel together. He didn't need me to say it—Marlon knew. His faith in that loving hand was strong. Then I said that it looked to me as though Rachel hadn't reached that place yet. But she would, when it was *Gott's wille* to reveal that to her."

Susanna was silent, but her whole being seemed to be listening. She'd even toned down her gaze to a lower tempera-ture, for which he was thankful. Malena was like this, too, when something was really important to her. It was quite a job keeping up with women like this—women like his grand-mother—who felt so much and weren't able to hide it.

"Then he said he wanted to propose, but was afraid she'd turn him down. Choose Luke instead of him. I couldn't do much about that, but I could advise him to wait on the Lord. Wait until He revealed the right time."

"How did he know when that was?"

Reuben smiled. "Well, that was between him and *Gott*, but it wasn't long. Maybe a couple of weeks. He proposed, and Rachel accepted. And after that there was only one man in her life."

Susanna reared up. "Not if you talk to her. Apparently she had feelings for Luke even after she married Dat!"

"Well, feelings aren't faucets," he said mildly. "They don't turn off and on or run hot or cold just because we want them to."

"That's what they both say," she mumbled, subsiding. He could practically see her hackles lying down again.

"They both married the one person *Gott* intended for them," he said gently. "And now it seems as though *Gott*'s hand is at work again. I often think the Almighty has a sense of humor. Or maybe it's just that His mercy endures forever. Isn't it quite a thing that He brought her and Luke back to the valley after all this time ... at the *same* time?"

"It's quite a thing, all right." But the intensity, the indignation, had gone out of her tone. "I still think it was horrible of her to cheat on Dat."

"But that was between my brother and Rachel. Not between you and Rachel," he said gently. "He doesn't need you to fight for him, *Liewi*. If there was any fighting, it was all done and forgiven long ago."

"Wholehearted," Susanna murmured. Then she glanced at him. "I should be mad at you for standing up for her and not me."

"Hearts are a little more complicated than that," he said, reaching around her shoulders to give her a one-armed hug. "Feelings are complicated, too. But what isn't complicated is how much you loved your *dat*. I did, too. And so did your mother. Marlon was easy to love, I think. It was one of his gifts."

Her mouth trembled, and she tilted into his shoulder, her face buried in his shirt as she began to cry. "I miss him so much."

"I know. And there's no law that says you have to stop. I doubt Rachel has stopped missing him, either." When she didn't argue, only sniffled and scrubbed her tears away with the flat of her hand, he dipped his oar in the water again. "I guess you have to ask yourself whether you want your *mamm* to be alone the rest of her life, missing your *dat*? Or now that you might have seen the hand of *Gott* in all this, do you think you ought to let her work out His will?"

"You really think that's what it is?"

He gazed up into the branches above their heads, the leaves the fresh green of spring that was his favorite color. The leaves that protected the fruit … fruit that would swell and grow and become something to feed and sustain. "I don't doubt it for a minute, *Liewi*. That's what faith is. Seeing the hand of God at work, being willing for it, and at last, rejoicing in it."

"Even when sometimes you wish it would work somewhere else?"

He chuckled. "Especially then."

With a sigh, she said, "*Denki*, Onkel Reuben. I might not like some of what you said, but I can't fight the truth of it."

Her head lay on his shoulder now in just the way he'd seen it on her father's when the two families had visited. So he did what Marlon would often do. He kissed her forehead.

"*Kumm, Liewi*. Let's go on down. Maybe you'd like to stay for the day and visit with your cousins?"

She considered it for a moment. "*Neh*, if someone can take me into town, I'd best go home. We're opening in three days, and I've left Mamm with all the laundry and cleaning to do."

Companionably, they left the orchard and walked down to the house. And while Malena wrapped up a quilt she wanted to offer the Rose Garden Quilt Shop on consignment, Reuben went out on the deck, where Naomi was pegging out the laundry on the line. He wrapped his arms around her from behind and hugged her.

"What is this for?" she murmured, kissing him under the ear.

"For being the one *Gott* wanted for me," he murmured back.

He left her smiling, and loped down the stairs to the barn. He saddled Chrysanthemum, feeling as though he'd already done a full day's work. And it wasn't even eight o'clock.

Wild Rose Amish Inn

When they'd first moved in, Tobias had set up a pole at one end of Rachel's future garden and mounted a pulley wheel on it, then strung her washing line between it and the deck outside the door at the end of the family corridor. As she pegged out laundry, she kept one eye on her work and the other on the road. She felt almost breathless, as though anticipation, fear, and hope were all pressing on her lungs.

Hitched to the Circle M buggy, Hester clip-clopped past and the breath went out of her in a rush.

"They're here!" she called to Luke, who was raking the soil in the garden, even though he didn't have to. Still keeping his distance after last night.

But she couldn't think about last night—the sweetness of his kiss—the strange sense that they had come full circle. Because unless some miracle had occurred over at the ranch, Susanna would be in a state of mind that would make it necessary for her to walk circumspectly. Follow Luke's example. See the lie of the land before speaking or acting. Because if her girl could walk five miles in the middle of the night, she could certainly find her way to Libby and the eastbound train. Rachel was not about to do anything that would force that to happen.

The buggy came to a stop in their parking lot, and Rachel hurried around the corner to the front. She was just in time to wave at Malena, who clearly had another errand, for she didn't get out, only waved back and called *"Guder mariye!"* She shook the reins over Hester's back and departed.

Susanna climbed the steps and Rachel met her at the top, gathering her into a hug. "I was so worried."

"I know. I'm sorry," Susanna whispered.

"Are you all right?"

She nodded. "I think so. It will take me a couple of days to think it all through. But for right now, I—I'd like to talk to you and Luke. Together. Please."

This was not the face of a happy woman. Her daughter looked almost on the point of tears. What had gone on out there?

With a feeling of dread, Rachel fell in beside her and they walked out to the scene of the crime—*neh*. She would not think that way. Kissing Luke had not been a crime. It had seemed like the next step on the path they were walking. The step that had changed their direction so that instead of passing by and leaving one another behind, they now walked side by side.

Luke leaned on his rake as they approached, his eyes shadowed under the brim of his straw hat. "I'm glad you're home safe, Susanna."

"I was never not safe," she said. "Though it was pretty dark on the highway this morning."

Rachel stifled the urge to demand what had possessed her to do such a thing. Because that would not be productive, and besides, the risk of danger was already over and done with.

"I've been doing some thinking out here," Luke said, "and I've made a few decisions."

This was news to Rachel.

She must have looked startled, because he said, "I didn't talk them over with you, Rachel, because they seemed right to me at the time, and still do. Susanna, I know how you feel about me. I've said what I could, but I'm not going to force any woman to change her mind, especially not you. I've decided that ... the best thing for me to do is to take another job. To move on."

Rachel's stomach plunged and her entire being cried out, *No!*

"I'm told that a foreman's job has come open on the Keim place, on the other side of the valley. I'd have preferred it to be in the western church district, but it can't be helped. I called Josiah before I left this morning and offered my services."

If Rachel had had a hard time breathing before, it was nothing to the way she felt now. She could hardly drag air into her lungs, she was so shocked and hurt.

Leave! He couldn't leave. Not the district, not the Inn. Not *her*.

For in that breath between one dreadful sentence and the next, she had realized with perfect clarity the state of her own heart.

She loved Luke Hertzler.

And not with a girl's foolish, self-involved love. Hers was the love of a woman who had known sorrow, and joy, and pain, too. A love that could encompass his sorrow and soothe his pain even as he learned how to feel joy again while they walked their path. Together, they would learn each other's funny quirks and tell over their stories, so that the future would contain the past as well as the present.

She must speak, before Susanna did.

"I've been making some decisions, too," her daughter said.

Ach, neh. Neh. Mei Gott, hilfe mich! She's going to leave us. Don't let her go all the way to the other side of the continent. Surely there is a way to—surely—

"I spent a long while with Onkel Reuben up in the orchard at the Circle M."

This was so completely the last thing she'd expected her to say that the panicked gabbling of prayer in Rachel's mind was abruptly silenced.

"And he helped me see that—that I haven't been fair. How many times has *Gott* thrown my sins into the sea of forgetfulness, never to be cast up to me again?" She answered her own question, since neither Rachel or Luke could manage a word. "Lots of times. And what have I been doing this past week? Holding the sins of the past—if that's what they even were—against both of you." Susanna took a shuddering breath, and raised her head to look Luke in the face. "It's not my place to tell you what to do, Luke. If you've arranged for another job, then that's your business. But before you go—Mamm, I'm saying this to you, too—I hope you will forgive me. I've been horrible to both of you, and I'm sorry."

With an inarticulate cry, Rachel flung her arms around her daughter and burst into tears. With the broken sentences coming out of her mouth, she wasn't even making sense, but Susanna knew how to make sense of love. And when the two of them had got their breath back, Luke held out both hands to Susanna, palm up like an offering, or a help.

She pulled on them and to his obvious surprise, he found himself in a hug. Through her tears, Rachel had to smile at

Susanna—as sudden and impulsive in generosity as she was in dislike.

"Forgive me?"

"Always," he said hoarsely. "And I haven't heard back from Josiah about the job. I'm sure he's got prospects standing in line."

"So you won't go? You'll stay with us and make my mother happy?"

Luke released her and looked over her shoulder at Rachel. "If she'll let me."

"Well, you two just talk it over," Susanna said firmly. "I believe I have a load of laundry to do."

The human tornado hurried across the lawn, leaving Rachel feeling as though she'd been spun around and set down in a completely different world. A world where the sun shone warm on her shoulders, and the sweet smell of the land rose up in promise, and, like wildflowers and hay, possibility was springing up all around her.

Luke gazed at her, the bemused expression on his face probably a lot like the one on her own. "That girl takes some getting used to."

"There are no half measures with Susanna," she said, a little breathlessly. "Did you mean it? You'll stay with us?"

He took a step closer and gathered her hands into his. "I'll stay. You're the reason I crossed a couple of states and risked the wrath of all your children, Rachel. Like I said before, wherever you are is my home. My heart. My refuge from the storm."

"And you were my secret room," she confessed. "I locked the door on you, but now I have a whole heart to welcome you into, with no secret doors. No closed ones, either."

He folded her into his arms, and with his head bowed on

her shoulder, his chest jerked in a way that told her he was holding back tears. Not of grief this time. But the kind that washed away the past, and began his lessons in joy.

"I love you," he whispered.

"And I love you. A different kind of love than before. But my whole heart is filled with it."

And when he kissed her, it was a different kind of kiss. The kind that showed his heart was filled with love—and more than that, with new purpose. Because both of them were sure in the knowledge that the *gut Gott* had brought them together again ... this time, for ever.

EPILOGUE
WILD ROSE AMISH INN

Friday, May 20, 3:00 p.m.

SUSANNA GLANCED NERVOUSLY at Mamm as they stood together at the front door. Just below, two big ceramic pots stood on either side of the steps, filled with blooming wild roses. In the patio area to the right, Sunny the hen introduced the chicks to the wonders of the dust bath, now that Luke had pruned back the blackberry bushes to within an inch of their lives. Over at the garden, Luke was hoeing furrows, the regular motion of the hoe somehow relaxing, though Susanna knew from experience it was hard, hot work. She smoothed her apron over her skirts as the black extended-cab pickup rolled slowly over their bridge and into the parking lot, where it seemed to take up almost the whole thing.

It was opening day. And these were their first guests.

Four men clambered out, hauling backpacks and duffel bags and the metal tubes that contained their fly rods. They stood, looking around them—the lawn, the Inn, the mountains that rose majestically in the distance. Then they saw Susanna and Mamm, and headed over in a bulky procession.

"*Wilkumm* to the Wild Rose Amish Inn," Mamm said with a smile. "I'm Rachel, and this is my daughter Susanna. Come on in."

For as nervous as she'd been this morning, Mamm was calm now, showing them the keeping room and the dining room, where a plate sat on the table piled with chocolate chip cookies baked so recently you could still smell the sweetness throughout the house. One of the men breathed it in.

"I'll show you to your rooms upstairs and you can settle in, then feel free to have some coffee and cookies and roam around the property."

"I understand there's no TV? No radio? And nowhere to charge our phones?" one of them asked as they climbed the stairs. "That's what the website said."

"You say that like it's a bad thing," one of the others retorted. "A week without work hounding me day and night? I'm all over it."

"You won't miss the first two," Susanna heard Mamm say. "Our creek opens tomorrow. You can fish right on the property and then come in to a big hot breakfast."

"Paradise," said the third with a sigh of happiness.

"And we have a a charging station in the mud room that's powered by our generator. You can charge phones and computers there—though I warn you there's no—no—"

Poor Mamm! She could never remember the words for things that were so necessary to the *Englisch*. "Wi-fi," Susanna called up the stairwell. "But the signal from the feed store reaches to the edge of their parking lot, so if you need to, you can go over there."

"I didn't even *bring* my computer," the second man said. "Are you kidding? I'm here for the fish."

Susanna took a deep breath. This would be a success. These men would tell their friends—maybe even post pictures on social media. Two women were coming in later today for the fishing, as well, and last night they'd had a call from a pair of newlyweds camping by the lake, who'd discovered too late that you really did have to lock up your food. Bears had happily demolished their campsite and they'd taken refuge in their car. At that point, money had become no object and they'd grabbed the room without question.

A buggy rattled over their bridge and Susanna glanced at the clock. Right on time.

She went outside just as the twins leaped out of Sylvia Keim's buggy and raced over to say hi to Luke. Sylvia leaned out the open door as Susanna walked up.

"Only a week of school left," Sylvia said with a grin as the twins ran for the patio, clearly just having been informed that the baby chicks were out. "I'm going to miss those two. I've enjoyed our trips back and forth."

"And Tobias is so grateful. It's been quite the operation, getting them to school and back every day now that we're living in the east district."

"It's been my pleasure. I see your guests have arrived. Did everything go smoothly?"

"So far," Susanna allowed. "I'm beginning to think no television and no wi-fi are bonuses for sportsmen. Fishing is as much an escape from their jobs as it is a sport or a way to stock the freezer."

Sylvia laughed. "Dat has found a way to combine fishing with ranching. He calls it providing for the family. I call it enjoying himself way too much—and when my brothers are here, it's a regular jamboree."

"I hope it's all right with him that Luke declined the foreman's job," Susanna said, shading her eyes from the sun. "You heard about him and Mamm?"

"I did, when I stopped at the Circle M. My goodness, it has certainly been the year for romance in the valley, hasn't it?" Her eyes did not meet those of Susanna, instead ranging over the neat lines of the Inn, with its welcoming wraparound porch and the new pots of roses. Her mouth looked almost sad.

"I suppose it has."

"As for Luke, my father understands," Sylvia said, recovering from her momentary abstraction. "He's needed here at the Inn, in more ways than one. And Dat did hire a foreman. A new man, just come to the valley, but with lots of experience. *And* ... he's *single*."

In the very depths of Susanna's being, a single note of alarm rang like a deep-throated bell.

"He says he used to work for you, which Dat really appreciated. It's nice for a new member of the *Gmay* to know people in a new place, don't you think? Like you folks having family here at the Circle M. It's an extra kind of welcome."

Susanna had lost the ability to concentrate on what Sylvia was saying. Her whole body had gone cold. "We—we've had a couple of foremen over the years," she managed, her mouth dry. "What's his name?"

"Stephen Kurtz," Sylvia said. "He's in his mid-twenties, so too young for me. Nice eyes, though." She laughed again. "Please don't tell him I said that."

Susanna didn't plan on it. In fact, she didn't plan on going to the Keim place ever again, other than for the annual visit allowed by the rotation of Sunday services from home to home.

She barely had the sense to wave good-bye as Sylvia turned the horse and it trotted out of the lot.

Stephen. Here in the Siksika. On the Keim place.

This couldn't be happening.

For the first time, she wished she really had bought that train ticket to Chicago and points east. Because safely on a little island on the other side of the continent, she would never have to face Stephen Kurtz again. Never have to remember the moment that haunted her.

When she'd been fool enough to offer her heart.

When he'd refused it, handing it back as though it meant nothing.

Her poor heart ... that despite everything, would always be his.

THE END

AFTERWORD
A NOTE FROM ADINA

I hope you've enjoyed the seventh book about the Miller family, launching this new miniseries about Rachel Miller and her family. If you subscribe to my newsletter, you'll hear about new releases in the series, my research in Montana, and snippets about quilting and writing and chickens—my favorite subjects!

I hope you'll join me by subscribing at:
https://www.subscribepage.com/shelley-adina.

Turn the page for a glossary of the Pennsylvania Dutch words used in this book. But first, here's a sneak peek at Susanna's book, *The Amish Cowboy's Mistake*, book eight of The Amish Cowboys of Montana series!

THE AMISH COWBOY'S MISTAKE © ADINA SENFT

When the past walks back into your life ...

Susanna Miller had her doubts when her mother bought a dilapidated historic inn in Mountain Home, Montana. But now the family has brought it back to life as the Wild Rose Amish Inn, and Susanna is helping to run it and show their guests some good Amish hospitality. She has barely settled in to her new life when she learns to her horror that Stephen Kurtz has hired on as foreman at a neighboring ranch. Once, he'd been their foreman. Once, he'd been the man of her dreams. But he'd walked away without even a good-bye ... leaving her rejected, brokenhearted, and alone.

It's already too late to run

Stephen Kurtz had thought Susanna Miller would be safely married to someone else by now. Someone far away. So it's a shock to move to the Siksika Valley and find her not only close at hand, but still single and as beautiful as ever. If not for his commitment to his employer, he'd find another job as far from the valley as he can get. But when the old attraction between them begins to sparkle, he's forced to admit that walking away for the best of reasons was the worst mistake he ever made. Is it too late to rekindle Susanna's love—or is his heart's sweet home lost to him forever?

The Montana Millers. They believe in faith, family, and the land. They'll need all three when love comes to Mountain Home!

GLOSSARY

Spelling and definitions from Eugene S. Stine, *Pennsylvania German Dictionary* (Birdboro, PA: Pennsylvania German Society, 1996).

Words used:

Aendi: auntie

Bischt du okay? Are you okay?

Boppli(n): baby, babies

Bruder: brother

Daadi: grandfather

Daadi Haus: grandfather house

Dat: Dad

deemiedich: humble

Demut: humility

denki: thanks

Dochsder: daughter

Dochsdere: daughters

Eck: corner, esp wedding table

Englisch: not-Amish people, English language

der Herr: the Lord

Grischdaag: Christmas

Gmay: congregation, church body

Gott: God

Grossdaadi: great-grandfather

Gross Gmay: Communion

Grossmammi: great-grandmother

Guder owed: Good afternoon/evening

Guder mariye: Good morning

Guder nacht: Good night

gut: good

Ischt okay? Is it okay?

ja: yes

Kaffee: coffee

Kapp: women's prayer covering

Kind, Kinner: child, children

kumm mit: come along

Liewi, Liewe: dear, dears

Maedsche(r): girl, girls

Mamm: Mom

Mammi: Grandma

Mann: man

mei: my

mei Fraa: my wife

mei Sohn: my son

Mei Vater, hilfe mich. My Father, help me.

Narre: idiots

narrisch: crazy

neh: no

Neuwesitzer(n): side-sitter(s), the bridal couple's supporters

Nix? Is it not?

Onkel: uncle

Ordnung: discipline, or standard of behavior and dress unique to each community

Ordnungs Gmay: Council Meeting

Schweschder(e): sister(s)

Sohn: son

Uffrohr : uproar

Wie geht's? How's it going?

wunderbaar: wonderful

Youngie: young people

Keys of Heaven

Balm of Gilead

The Longest Road

The Highest Mountain

The Sweetest Song

The Heart's Return (novella)

Smoke River

Grounds to Believe

Pocketful of Pearls

The Sound of Your Voice

Over Her Head

Glory Prep (faith-based young adult)

Glory Prep

The Fruit of My Lipstick

Be Strong and Curvaceous

Who Made You a Princess?

Tidings of Great Boys

The Chic Shall Inherit the Earth

ABOUT THE AUTHOR

USA Today bestselling author Adina Senft grew up in a plain house church, where she was often asked by outsiders if she was Amish (the answer was no). She holds a PhD in Creative Writing from Lancaster University in the UK. Adina was the winner of RWA's RITA Award for Best Inspirational Novel in 2005, a finalist for that award in 2006, and was a Christy Award finalist in 2009. She appeared in the 2016 documentary film *Love Between the Covers*, is a popular speaker and convention panelist, and has been a guest on many podcasts, including Worldshapers and Realm of Books.

She writes steampunk adventure and mystery as Shelley Adina; and as Charlotte Henry, writes classic Regency romance. When she's not writing, Adina is usually quilting, sewing historical costumes, or enjoying the garden with her flock of rescued chickens.

Adina loves to talk with readers about books, quilting, and chickens!
www.adinasenft.com
adinasenft@comcast.net

facebook.com/adinasenft

x.com/shelleyadina

pinterest.com/shelleyadina

bookbub.com/authors/adina-senft

instagram.com/shelleyadinasenft

Made in United States
North Haven, CT
05 April 2024

50939330R00145